BROKEN TULIPS

Book 2 in the Blue Rose Series

Written By

Julie Thorpe

Julie Thorpe

This series of books are written in loving memory of my parents whom are no longer with us.

They encouraged me to write and to read many books and this is dedicated to them.

This is a work of fiction.

Names, characters, organisations, places, events and incidences are either products of the author's imagination or used fictitiously.

Copyright 2019 by Julie Thorpe.

All rights reserved.

No part of this book may be reproduced, or stored in a retrieval system, or transmitted in any form or by any means, electronic, mechanical, photocopying, recording, or otherwise without the express written permission of the publisher.

Publisher: Julie Thorpe Publishing.

CHAPTER ONE.

My sister was dead.

We had arranged the funeral between us, helping to alleviate the pain from the added pressure of organising a funeral but it was the hardest thing I know I've ever had to do. Cal, the man that was supposed to marry my sister, was in bits but he did his best to hold himself together so that he could look after their daughter, Lily. My beautiful niece had lost her mother on the same day that she was born but we had taken lots of photographs of them together so that we could show Lily when she grew up and could appreciate it. For now, we had to actually get through the funeral and I was a mess. Lord knows how Cal must have been feeling. He'd lost the love of his life, his soulmate and anyone who looked at him could see the raw pain on his face at the loss.

"Jacob! Are you nearly ready? We've got to get to the house!" I called out. Honestly, my husband infuriated me at times. He knew this was an extremely important day and yet, I was having to hurry him up because he was so laid back and kept saying there was plenty of time. Admittedly, there was enough time yes, I agree, but I needed to be there for my family. My sisters' death had been hard. She was my last living relative as we'd lost both of our parents already and now that my sister was gone, I had a keen sense of loneliness always surrounding me. I know I had Jacob but it wasn't the same as having family around whom I'd grown up with.

"I'm coming now!" Jacob called back to me, huffing in annoyance as he stomped down the stairs to where I stood.

I stared at him in disbelief. He hadn't done his shirt up, his tie was slung over his shoulder and his feet were still bare as he padded across the hall into the living room. I followed after him.

"You're not even dressed! Can you please hurry up? If you're not ready in the next ten minutes then I'm going without you!"

Jacob glanced back at me, rolling his eyes as he bent over to put on his socks.

"Will you please relax? I'll be ready so there's no need for all of this nagging."

I couldn't believe my ears. I felt like I was dealing with some sullen teenager who'd just been told off.

"In case you've somehow forgotten Jacob, we're burying my sister today. I know the two of you weren't fond of each other but she meant a lot to me and I'd appreciate it if you could try and be supportive for me today instead of annoying me with every thing that you do. You're my husband and you may not realise this, but I need you. OK? I need you today," I told him, the fight going out of me as I spoke those last words and tears welled up in my eyes. Why did he always make things so hard?

Jacob stood from where he sat and came over to me, wrapping his arms around me to pull me in close against him. I closed my eyes and breathed deeply, trying to calm myself.

"Ssh, don't cry babe," Jacob whispered into my hair, "I'm sorry, I don't mean to annoy you. I'm here for you, you know I am. I love you Ellen and I'll always support you."

I raised my head to gaze into his eyes, seeing the earnest expression facing me. I sighed.

"I love you too, Jacob. I'm sorry if I was nagging you but I just need today to go well. You know?"

He nodded his head as I pulled away from him.

"I get it babe, I truly do. I'll be with you the whole time and if you need to cry or to be held, I'll be right by your side. OK?" he reassured me as he quickly slid his shirt buttons into their holes and tucked the tails into his trousers.

A few minutes later and he'd put his tie on, put his black shoes on and picked his jacket up to finish off the look. Finally, we were ready to leave.

Luckily, we only lived in the next village over from Cal so we made it there within five minutes.

As I walked in, I could hear Cal crying and Lily was screaming.

"Please Little Bun, please calm down. Daddy needs you to stop crying for just a few minutes…please? I'm sorry Daddy's crying, but Daddy is sad today."

I felt my heart swell at Cal's heart breaking words and strode in, going straight over to him to let him know we were there.

"Cal?" I spoke softly so as not to make him jump, "I'm here with Jacob now. Do you want me to take Lily for a cuddle for a bit to give you some space and time to compose yourself?"

Cal looked woefully up at me and I had to do my best not to burst into tears right along with him. The pain in his eyes was unmistakeable, raw agony reflecting back at me. A lump formed in my throat which I had to swallow away, trying to keep my own composure as I took in the sight of the father of my niece. The poor man. I was hurting sure, but I couldn't imagine how hard it must be to lose the person that I loved and had made plans with. To know that the child they'd created would never know her mum was horrible.

He handed the baby over to me silently, giving

me a small tight smile to show his appreciation through his tears and once I'd taken a hold of her, he stood up and stalked off upstairs. I gazed down at my gorgeous niece, smiling as I noticed that her eyes were the same as her mothers' whilst I rocked her in my arms to calm her.

After a mere few minutes, the baby girl quieted down, gurgling instead as I pulled funny faces at her as it appeared to amuse her. I felt someone creep up behind me, appearing in my peripheral vision.

"Is there anything you'd like me to do babe?" Jacob muttered into my ear, gazing down at the little bundle in my arms. I shook my head.

"No, I'm alright thanks. But could you check on Cal? I really don't think he's coping."

Jacob agreed before ambling away to follow Cal up the stairs. I turned my attention back to Lily, whom was also called Little Bun as that was the nickname my sister had given to her whilst she was still a 'bun in the oven.' She'd got chubby little cheeks and a toothless smile, a small spattering of brown hair was sprouting on her head and she was so petite that she was simply adorable.

I pulled another face at her, smiling to myself as she gave me a little smile. She had such a lovely temperament, just like her mum used to. I felt a tear filling up in my eye as I thought about my sister. I still couldn't believe that we were burying her this day. She had been younger than me and to have lost her to a brain tumour had been devastating. It had been a few weeks since she died but I was still reeling from the fact that we'd lost her from our lives. What would I do without her?

A short time later, Cal and Jacob reappeared, dressed and ready for the funeral that we were about to embark upon. A few of Cal's family members and some of our friends came to join us at the house before the funeral began so that they could share in our grief and show their support.

When the hearse arrived with my sister in her coffin and the people from the funeral home came to announce their arrival, we all went outside to begin the procession walk to the church. The church itself was only a couple of minutes up the road but we took our time, moving slowly along the road as we followed the hearse to the church. Once we reached it, we waited for the pallbearers to lift the coffin onto their shoulders so that we could follow them in.

Cal led the way after the coffin with Lily fast asleep in his arms. I followed behind him with Jacob whilst everyone else remained behind us, keeping a respectful distance from us. I was grateful for the fact that Amber had so many people there to pay their respects to her life, offering their condolences to Cal and to myself.

The service itself was lovely. I knew exactly what would happen with which hymns that would be sung and prayers that would be told as I'd helped with the organisation of the service but to actually witness everything coming together properly, knowing that it was all going to plan, made me feel calmer. I hadn't realised just how worried I'd been over it until we were sat there in the pews.

When we got to the speech that Cal had written for the service, the dam of tears that I'd been holding back finally broke free. His words were so touching that I couldn't help myself. I cried and cried, holding on tightly to Jacob's hand as I did. He was my anchor to get me through.

When the service ended, Amber's coffin was carried outside to the graveyard, the plot next to our parents to be her final destination. She'd always told me that that was where she wanted to be buried if she died before me so we had chosen to fulfil her wish. Looking at the headstone for my parents, knowing that my sister was now joining them, made hot tears leak from my eyes afresh. I couldn't believe we were burying my baby sister! Why was this world so cruel? Why couldn't she have lived to be old and grey? To see her child grow up? To have a happy life with Cal? I felt almost guilty for still being alive, for being able to do all of the things she no longer could. I was her big sister, it should've been me who died first. It wasn't fair!

Broken Tulips

After the final words for the service, Amber's coffin was lowered into the ground, making the whole thing sink in that it was final. This was it. Amber was gone from us with only our memories for comfort.

All of the people who had been to the service began to head off towards the local pub which was where we were holding the wake. By the time Jacob and I decided to go and join them all, there was only us and Cal left with baby Lily in his arms. I walked over to him and touched him gently on the arm.

"Cal? Do you want to come with us to the pub? I'd rather not leave you on your own."

"Sure, yeah. I'll come," he replied dully, the heartache he was feeling plain to hear in his voice.

He turned to walk with us as we headed to the wake.

Everybody else was already in there, drinks in hand, reminiscing about my little sister. It was nice to hear the stories they were telling about her. It was clear to me that she had been well loved by all of the locals which was exactly what I'd needed to see on this day.

We spent the rest of the afternoon and evening drinking and talking about Amber, celebrating her life that had cruelly been cut short. At about seven, Cal told us he was going home to put Lily to bed. He thanked everyone for attending before he left, reassuring me that he would be alright. I told him to call me if he wasn't, although when I turned to see Jacob's face, I half wished I hadn't said anything. Jacob looked like he was angry although I couldn't for the life of me think why he would be. I hadn't done anything wrong.

Needless to say, we left shortly after that, arriving home in silence. I had a prickly feeling in my gut, wondering to myself why he would be angry that I'd offered my support to Cal. If Amber had survived and married the man like they'd planned, then he would be my brother in law. I couldn't see the problem.

"Jacob? Did I do something wrong?" I asked tentatively. I figured I might as well get this out of the way now.

Jacob sighed, scrubbing a hand over his face before he replied.

"No. No you didn't babe. I'm sorry. I just find you so gorgeous and sexy that whenever you talk to someone else, I find I get a bit jealous. I hope you forgive me."

Really? This had all been because he was jealous? I felt slightly dubious but as it had been such an emotionally draining day, I decided to let it go.

"Of course I do, but there's nothing to be jealous of. I'm with you and that's how it will stay. We're married. I'd never do anything like that to you. Shall we watch a movie? I could do with a night to just relax after today. What do you say?"

I hoped he'd say yes. That way we could sit on the sofa, snuggle up and watch a film together without having to worry about anything else for a little while.

Jacob's mouth twitched as he thought about it, smiling at me eventually as he agreed. Phew! Thank the Lord for that. I didn't know what had gotten into him lately but Jacob had been acting weird. I didn't know if it was because of everything that had happened with Amber or with the things that had been happening at his job, but he had certainly begun to change from when we'd first gotten together. I decided to forget about it for now. We were going to have a movie night to relax and unwind after an emotionally hard day.

Chapter Two.

A couple of months passed.

One Saturday morning, the sun was shining and I decided to go and visit Cal and Lily. Jacob was at a training day for work so I was by myself. I got into my car and drove over to Cal's house, pulling up outside and sitting there for a few minutes.

It had been a few months since Amber had died but this house had been hers for a long time. Every time I came to the house, I half expected to walk in and find her sitting on the sofa, laughing with Cal. It was a hard reality to remember with clarity each time that she was gone. I took in a deep breath before getting out of my car to steady my nerves and slammed the door shut behind me. I noticed the weeds in the garden were starting to look a bit overrun and figured that Cal probably hadn't had time to sort it what with looking after a newborn baby. Maybe I would offer to tidy it up for him. I strolled up to the front door, ringing the doorbell then waited. My eyes trailed down to the ground, taking in the mess of the small porch way. There were small stones, leaves and various bits that inevitably came in from off the bottoms of peoples shoes. I'd never really noticed it before but there was so much now that it was noticeable. I frowned to myself. Was Cal struggling more than I'd thought?

My thoughts were suddenly interrupted by the front door opening.

"Ellen! Hi! How are you doing? Come on in," Cal welcomed me, moving aside and holding the door open for me, his bedraggled appearance concerning me.

I moved past him into the hall and waited for him to close the door behind me, before we moved into the living room. I took a seat on the sofa and studied the dishevelled man as he placed himself in the chair opposite to me. His shirt was creased and untucked, his jeans appeared as though they could use a wash and the dark circles under his eyes indicated a lack of sleep of massive proportions. He scrubbed a hand over his chin as I took a quick glance about me. I couldn't see the baby anywhere.

"Where's Little Bun today? Sleeping?" I asked casually, thinking she must be upstairs in her cot. Cal shook his head.

Julie Thorpe

"No actually. My mum and dad came round earlier and have taken her to stay with them for the night. She's going to be back tomorrow. Sorry, did you come to see her?"

"Oh no, don't worry!" I assured him, "I came to see you just as much as I was coming to see her....How are you doing?"

Cal shrugged his shoulders nonchalantly.

"I'm doing okay. And yourself?"

"I'm alright but I'm going to be honest with you Cal. You don't look like you're doing okay. Why haven't you told me you've been struggling? I know this is all a huge adjustment for you but we are all here to help you."

I hoped I was getting through to him but frankly, I truly didn't know if I was. We had all told him that we would help him but he'd obviously not listened to us much. I watched as he hung his head, the shame showing upon his face.

"I do know you will all help me. To be honest, I'm not struggling with being a dad. I love Little Bun to bits but I'm missing Amber so much it hurts. I take care of Little Bun but forget to look after myself I guess. Please don't think badly of me," Cal muttered, not once looking me in the eye.

"Cal, I don't think badly of you! I'm worried about you is all. If you need me to help with things around the house or if you want me to babysit so that you can do the things you need then all you've got to do is ask. Honestly, that's it. I'm always going to help you if I can," I told him earnestly, my heart lifting as he finally raised his gaze to my face, "now, I apologise if I sound bossy but go and have a shower or a bath and do some grooming. I'll do your washing and tidy up down here. If you want a nap, go have one...and before you protest, I'm not taking no for an answer. Understood?"

Cal stared at me in disbelief for a moment before visibly relaxing, his shoulders sagging as he sighed.

"A shower and a nap would be nice I must admit," he replied quietly, "you don't have to do the cleaning or anything though. I'm not asking you to do that."

"I know you're not. I'm offering. So go, do what you need to do and leave this to me," I told him boldly, taking him by the arm to steer him in the direction of the stairs.

He went without uttering another word, much to my relief.

I turned around once he had gone and began. I gathered up all of his clothes (and called up to him to throw the rest down the stairs for me which he did) and put them in the washing machine to get clean. Next, I set about cleaning his kitchen, sweeping and mopping the floor, and putting things away that had been left out on the countertops before moving back into the living room.

I tidied and dusted the room, putting things back into their places before pulling out the hoover to get any and all bits up from off the floor. I knew the sound of the hoover meant there was a chance that Cal would wake up if he'd nodded off but from how tired he had appeared, I knew he would drop straight back off again.

Eventually, I was finished with the living room, everything looking the way it should. I could hear that the washing machine had stopped so I took some time to empty it and place the clothes into the tumble dryer, hoping they would dry reasonably quickly so that I could iron them before I'd had enough of cleaning. Cleaning had never been something I enjoyed so doing it for someone else was a bit of a rarity, but it had needed doing. I'd promised my sister I would help her family as much as I was able to and if this was how I could help them, then so be it.

Once all of that was done, I took the hoover with me into the porch and proceeded to get up all of the bits in there that I had noticed when I'd first arrived. Glancing about, I was satisfied with what I'd achieved.

I returned the hoover to its hiding place, then

looked about me for some gloves. When Cal finally came back downstairs a couple of hours later, he found me in the front garden taking up his weeds.

"Ellen! You really don't need to do that," he chided, coming to stand beside me as I rose up to my feet from my knees.

"Pssh! Of course I do! I said I'd help so I am. Besides, I think that's the best I can do for now. I'm sweating!"

"Thanks for letting me know that," he chuckled at me as I led the way back into the house, taking my gloves off as we went. I laughed along with him. He certainly seemed to be in a better mood than when I'd first seen him. Who knew that a little bit of sleep and a hot shower would work so well? I gestured for Cal to sit down whilst I went into the kitchen to make us both a drink.

"Coffee?" I asked, pulling two cups out of the cupboard and proceeding to make the drinks before getting my reply. I knew it would be a yes.

"Yes please!" Cal called back to me, "the living room looks great! Thankyou so much for this, Ellen. I bet you've done the kitchen too haven't you?"

"Yeah I have but it's no problem so don't think any more about it," I finished making the drinks and took them back into the living room, handing him the coffee, "I've just got to iron your clothes and

I think you're all set for today. Although I haven't been upstairs yet."

Cal raised his hand up placatingly, smiling at me warmly.

"Honestly Ellen, I appreciate all of your help but don't do any more today. I'll do the ironing and clean upstairs in a bit. Like I say, I've got a night to myself tonight so I'll do those bits then I'll get to work on the book. I really do appreciate it though. Thankyou," he told me in a sincere manner.

I nodded my head to acknowledge what he'd said.

"Of course, anytime. I'm sorry if I'm being a bit pushy."

"Not at all," he reassured me, "I just don't expect you to tidy up after me. I promise you, I'll stay on top of things now. I've just let things slide more than I should have."

"OK. If you need me to babysit at all, then don't hesitate to ask me alright?" I told him, taking a sip of my own drink then.

We spent some time chatting to each other, catching up on things. He spoke to me about the book that he'd mentioned he'd work on. It was the one that Amber had been in the middle of writing before she'd died. She had made Cal promise to finish it whilst her literary agent would get it published for her and I must admit, I was intrigued to read it.

Broken Tulips

Cal had kept it under wraps so far but I knew that it was a personal story from Amber. I'd already told him I didn't mind waiting to read it as long as I did get to read it.

After a little while, I heard my phone vibrate to signal that I'd gotten a message come through. Pulling it out of my pocket, I glanced down and read the message. It was from Jacob.

"That's Jacob. He's home now so I guess I should get going," I said, standing up as I did so, "are you going to be alright?"

"Yes I'll be fine," Cal assured me, also standing up, "thankyou so much for what you've done today. I'll be sure to get you to babysit more so that I can keep on top of things. Now, go and have some fun with your husband. Enjoy the rest of your weekend."

I gave him a small smile and hugged him briefly, before heading out of the door to go home.

Jacob was standing in the kitchen when I arrived home, a cup of tea steaming in his hands as he turned to face me. He didn't appear happy.

"Where have you been?" he demanded, not bothering to say hello. Great, he was in one of *those* moods again. I hoped I could cheer him up so that we could enjoy the rest of our weekend together otherwise it wasn't going to be a pleasant couple of days. He'd been in a bad mood more often than not recently and I had no idea why. It had started to make me paranoid that I was doing something wrong, to the point that I had to remind myself that I wasn't and it was all on him.

"I was helping Cal," I replied, moving over to his side and bending down into the fridge to get a soda can out. I took a swig from the can as my husband glared at me.

"Why?"

"Because he's struggling Jacob. You were at work for your training day and I was bored so I originally went around to see Lily but she wasn't there. Cal looked bad, his clothes were a mess and the house was a mess and he was so obviously tired that I told him to go and have a nap whilst I tidied up for him. I didn't do much but it helped him in a small way," I watched the expression on his face as he clearly grew angrier, "I only did what Amber would have done if it were the other way around. If I had been the one who'd died and you'd been left behind on your own, I know she would have come round to help you too."

There, that was it. That was what I'd needed to say to calm him down.

Immediately, his face had softened and he took a step closer to me, wrapping one arm around my shoulders whilst he held his drink in his other one. He pressed a kiss against my cheek.

"Don't say that babe," he muttered, "I'm sorry Amber is gone but I'd hate it if it had been you. I'm sorry for getting angry over you being there, it's just been a bad day at work is all. That training was completely pointless! Please say you'll forgive me?"

He nuzzled his face against my neck, kissing me in the softness there. I closed my eyes and leaned into him, grateful that I'd said the right thing to change his mood. I couldn't have borne it if he'd been horrible all weekend.

"Of course I forgive you Jacob. I do wish I could do something to make things better for you at work. Hopefully spending the weekend with me will be good enough to cheer you up."

Jacob turned his body, placing his hands on the counter top behind me on either side of my body, encasing me in his arms. He must have put his tea cup down without my realising it. He bent his head after a moment, capturing my mouth in his swiftly, his lips warm against mine as he kissed me deeply, pushing me back against the counter as he did so. It was tender, a slow action that reminded me of when we'd first gotten together. Ah, my husband was definitely in a better mood now.

There had been something I'd wanted to talk to him about for a few weeks now and I figured this would be as good a time as any to say what I wanted to do. He broke the kiss, moving his face to my neck and trailing kisses across my collarbone.

"Jacob? Can I talk to you about something?" I asked softly as I ran my fingers through his blonde hair, hoping I could keep him distracted happily as I spoke to him. I'd discovered early on in our relationship that the best time to talk to him about something important was when he was distracted by kissing and everything else that went with that. It wasn't because he wouldn't listen at any other time but it was because he always seemed to be in a better mood and more amenable to listen to me without getting angry this way.

"Sure, what's up babe?" he asked, changing his position to kiss the other side of my neck and along to my shoulder.

"I've been thinking a lot about what I want to do with my life since we lost Amber and I've finally made a decision. I'd like to train to become a nurse."

Jacob stopped what he was doing and pulled back at that, his eyes boring into mine as he studied my face for a few moments. I waited, unsure of what he was going to say. Before Jacob and I had gotten together, I would have just gone and done it without telling anyone my plans until they were underway. However, now I was in a partnership and this education would probably cost money, I knew it was a decision that we needed to make together. It couldn't just be my decision anymore.

"A nurse huh?" Jacob asked, a thoughtful expression crossing over his features.

I nodded my head, remaining silent. I knew that would be the best course of action to take if I wanted a positive response. He seemed to think about it for a minute before he answered me.

"Sounds good to me babe. Yeah, go for it. If that's what you want to do then I'm behind you one hundred percent," he stated, giving me a broad smile in encouragement.

I felt relief course through my body at his words. Good, he wasn't going to stand in my way on this. I kissed him on the lips out of happiness that I was actually going to be able to go for my dream.

"Thankyou Jacob, I appreciate you supporting me on this," I told him sincerely, hoping he realised just how grateful I was.

He smiled down at me, his grey eyes sparkling in the light from above us.

"You're welcome. I know you probably feel more passionate about it because of everything that happened with your sister so I'll support you. You're my wife and I'd like to make you happy. Now, let me kiss you so I can show you how much I love you," he whispered into my ear, blowing against it as he knew it tickled me when he did that. I giggled as he took my chin in his hand, forcing my face up to meet his as his lips descended

Julie Thorpe

onto mine once more.

He was tender once more, moving his lips against mine in an almost leisurely manner and I sighed, tangling my fingers into his hair once again. His tongue licked along the seam of my mouth as he waited for me to open my mouth to his and surrender myself to him. I did as he wanted, closing my eyes as he deepened the kiss, his tongue exploring the inside of my mouth as if this were our first kiss. This was what I loved about him. The fact that when he kissed me, he could make it feel as though it were the first time all over.

His arms wrapped around my body, pulling me closer against him as his kiss grew more urgent. His hands tugged at the hem of my top, pulling it upwards until his fingers found my bra. Breaking free of the kiss, he yanked my top off over my head before returning his mouth to mine.

His fingers trailed slowly up my sides, feeling the soft skin of my body as I cupped my hands around his bottom to pull him closer towards me, kissing him back hungrily. Jacob was in a good mood and he *wanted* me. That didn't happen too often these days so I was going to enjoy whatever happened whilst it lasted. Hopefully, this would help to revive our marriage a little bit.

I felt his hands move to my back to take my bra in hand and untie it. I felt it the moment that the clasps came undone, as he slipped the straps from my shoulders and removed the scrap of material altogether, freeing me to his gaze and his touch. He took a globe in each hand then, caressing me as he pressed kisses against my neck, causing me to arch into him as my desire grew.

I trailed my fingers across his abdomen, pushing his shirt up so I could feel the taut muscles there. I groaned at his caresses, pushing his shirt up higher until he let go of me so that I could take it off of him. When it was off, I moved to his jeans, undoing them and sliding them down within seconds, my view of him still blocked by his boxers. He grinned wickedly at me then, pushing his boxers down in one motion and stepping free of them when they hit the ground.

My breath caught in my throat. He was still just as sexy to me as the day we had gotten together. I ogled him for a moment or two as he stood utterly naked in front of me and enjoyed the view.

"Do you mind?" he asked, a smile tugging at the corners of his lips.

"Not at all," I replied, keeping my gaze locked on him.

"I can't do much if you don't lose your jeans," Jacob told me, stepping close to me and playing with one breast lazily. I laughed at that before pushing my own jeans and pants down in one motion, stepping out of them and shoving them to the side with my foot.

"Happy now?" I asked, blushing slightly as he stared at my body, taking me all in.

"You've put on a bit of weight haven't you?" he muttered to himself, loud enough for me to hear him. Instantly, my desire was doused. What? Had I just heard him right?

"I beg your pardon?"

"I'm just saying you've put on a bit of weight. Not a lot, don't get me wrong but your body isn't what it used to be is it?" he stated, cocking his head to the side as he continued to stare at me.

Wow. I couldn't believe it. I wasn't exactly overweight and what with living my life and thinking I was happily married, I hadn't gone to the gym so much recently so I hadn't put on weight, I'd merely lost some of the tone I'd achieved at the gym...but to hear him say that, made me feel self-conscious of my body and not sexy at all.

I pulled away from him then as he leant forwards to kiss me, putting my hand up to his chest to push him away from me.

"I think you'll have to sort yourself out tonight. I've just lost any desire I had," I told him dully, bending and picking my clothes up from off the floor.

"Aw come on Ellen! Don't be like that! I still want

to make love to you, even if you're not as attractive as you used to be," he whined, trying to get closer to me again.

"Seriously? That's how you expect to get me to sleep with you? By insulting me?" I queried, shaking my head in total disbelief, "I'm going for a shower. Don't join me please. I'll see you later."

With that, I stalked off, holding my chin up as I clutched my clothes tightly against my chest as I fought to keep the tears at bay whilst I stalked off.

I heard him cursing to himself, cursing about how awful I was as a wife and the like. What had I done to make him behave like that towards me? Had I not done everything he wanted? And when had he started to think I wasn't as attractive as I used to be?

I had so many questions running through my mind but I shook them from me, stepping into the shower and letting the water cascade over me.

That's when I let the tears fall.

CHAPTER THREE.

The following day, Jacob informed me that he was going to go and play golf with his friends for the day. I simply shrugged my shoulders and turned away from him, waiting until he'd gone before I did anything else.

I was still smarting from the things he'd said to me the night before and the fact that he hadn't bothered to apologise to me hadn't helped. We'd barely spoken to each other for the rest of the night and then that morning, we'd spoken even less. I was so angry with him that I didn't trust myself not to say something that I would later regret. He had truly hurt my feelings and I wasn't yet ready to forgive him.

Once my horrible husband had left, I pulled my laptop out of its' case and placed it on my lap and turned it on. If I was going to become a nurse, I needed to discover what was required of me to do so. I spent the next couple of hours researching and reading up on what I would need to do. It appeared that I would need to do a nursing degree at a university but there were certain entry requirements before I could get into university so I decided to look those up also. I worked it out that I had some of the entry requirements but I would need to do an A-level course in Science to be able to apply so I went on to search for night classes at the local college to be able to do that.

I found that my local college did indeed do night classes for what I needed and that their customer service line was open at weekends so I decided to give them a call and see how I should apply.

The phone was answered within a few seconds by a pleasant sounding lady on the other end. She enquired as to what I was interested in doing so I told her and that it would help me to get into university for a nursing degree. She then proceeded to tell me about various things I might need and how else the college could help to which I gave her my email address so that she could send all of the information on to me for me to read through later. I thanked her before asking how I should apply for the course I wanted to do. To my relief, she told me that she could do it on the phone with me there and then.

I then spent the next half an hour, applying for the course I needed with the kind lady on the phone and when our conversation was finally over, I hung up the phone feeling rather pleased with myself.

I was finally doing something that I wanted to do and I owed it all to Amber. Without her, I would probably have not thought about entering the nursing world but I had seen how the nurses had helped my sister and I longed to help and provide

Julie Thorpe

comfort for others in their hours of need also.

Gazing about me, my smile faltered as I recalled how my husband had been with me. I wanted to share the news with him that I'd applied for night classes at the college to do my A-level course in Science, but at the same time, I didn't want to talk to him. So who else could I talk to?

It hit me a moment later. Cal! I picked my phone up again and dialled his number, waiting for him to answer.

"Hello?"

"Cal? Are you at home? Can I come and see you? I've got some news I'd like to share," I gushed, unable to hide my excitement in my voice.

I heard his chuckle on the other end of the phone.

"Sounds intriguing! Yes, of course, come on over. You know you're always welcome Ellen," he replied.

I hung up the phone and smiled to myself as I got myself sorted and dashed over to Cal's house. I parked my car outside on the pavement, noticing the silver car that stood behind Cal's on the driveway. Was someone else there? I felt anxious suddenly, hoping that I wouldn't be interrupting anything. I walked up the path to the house before ringing the doorbell.

The door opened for me to be greeted by Ryan,

Cal's brother.

"Oh. Hello Ryan, how are you?" I asked in surprise.

He grinned openly at me, stepping aside to let me into the house.

"Hi Ellen! I'm good, how are you? Cal said you were on your way over. Go on through to the living room, everyone's in there."

"Everyone?" I asked uncertainly, stepping slowly into the room. I was greeted by the sight of Cal, his parents Harry and Rachel and my beautiful niece, Lily. I relaxed immediately. I liked Cal's family, they had been a tremendously kind group of people and I was thankful that they had been there for Cal and Lily since Amber had passed away. Rachel even checked in on me occasionally to see how I was which was lovely for her to do.

They all smiled at me warmly when they saw I was there. Rachel stood up and came over to me straight away, wrapping her arms about me in a warm hug. I returned it, smiling at her as she stepped back again.

"Hi Rachel. Hi everyone," I greeted them all with a smile upon my lips.

Cal came over to me then with Lily in his arms. Lily was sleeping, her tiny fingers wrapped around Cal's thumb and I studied her sleeping form with pride. She grew to look more and more like Amber each day.

"Hi Ellen, come and join us. Would you like to stay for dinner?" he asked me, gesturing for me to sit in one of the seats.

"Oh no, thankyou. I'll have to go and cook for Jacob so I might as well eat with him," I replied as I sat down in the seat proffered to me.

Cal nodded his acknowledgment as everybody took their seats once more. Once he was settled, baby Lily comfortably within his arms upon his lap, he turned his gaze back to me.

"So, what is the good news you wanted to tell me?" he asked, watching me expectantly.

I blushed as I glanced around me, the hairs on my arm rising as Ryan took a seat next to me, his knee brushing gently against mine. Woah! Why on earth was I so aware of Cal's brother all of a sudden? I cleared my throat and moved away from Ryan discreetly before I replied.

"Um, well, it probably seems a bit silly to you all but I'm going back to college," I announced. I wasn't sure how else to say it so I just came out with it.

"College? Wow, well done you!" Cal exclaimed, giving me a broad smile.

"What are you going to be studying?" Ryan asked from my side, leaning in slightly closer to me, curiosity etched on his face. I glanced down at my hands nervously, speaking to them next with my head bowed as I didn't want to see their reactions when I told them.

"I'm going to be studying A level Science."

Stunned silence surrounded me at that. I lifted my eyes to see confusion on the majority of the faces peering back at me.

"Erm, can I ask why?" Ryan asked, appearing to be baffled by my choice of study. I tried to prevent the smile that was attempting to claim my lips.

"Yes. I'm studying it so that once I've passed, I can go to university. I'm planning to apply for a nursing degree as soon as I've got the examination results I need to be able to get in."

Gasps filled the room.

"You're going into nursing? Congratulations! Well done you for choosing to do something so wonderful," Rachel announced, clasping her hands together excitedly, "I bet Jacob must be pleased?"

My face fell at that and I glanced back down at my hands, twiddling my fingers around and around.

"He doesn't know yet actually," I replied, lifting my chin up and facing them once more, "I told him it was something I wanted to do but he doesn't know yet that I've applied for the course."

"How come?" Cal asked gently, his brows furrowing together at that.

"Well I only applied this morning and he's been out golfing all day," I told him nonchalantly, noticing his eyes narrowing at me. He shot a glance to his side, handing Lily over to his mum before standing up and turning back to me.

"Ellen? Do you mind coming up to the study with me? I need to show you something," he asked, waiting for me to stand and go up to the study where Amber and he tended to do their writing.

When we were in the room, Cal closed the door behind him before facing me, his expression grave.

"What's going on Ellen?"

"What do you mean?" I asked him innocently.

"There's something going on between you and Jacob isn't there? I could tell when you were talking downstairs that something isn't right," he told me.

I looked away, gazing about the room to prolong the silence between us. I should have realised that Cal would pick up on my anger at my husband. He was great at reading people. I strolled over to a shelf on the wall that housed a host of books that had all been written by my sister. I passed my hands gently over the spines of them, tracing her name with my fingers.

"We just had a fight is all Cal. Nothing to worry

about," I told him, moving over towards the table in front of the window.

I felt Cal come up behind me, stopping a mere few steps away from me.

"Ellen? Are you sure there is nothing else? Every time we speak about Jacob lately, there isn't much I hear that is good. You being Amber's sister, I feel like I should look out for you. Please would you tell me if something is wrong?" he pleaded quietly with me, his hand coming to a rest on my arm.

I sighed.

"Yes, of course I would Cal. You don't have to feel responsible for me though, I'm old enough to look after myself," I assured him, giving him a tight smile.

"I know you can take care of yourself Ellen, but I just want you to know that you don't have to deal with things by yourself. You're a part of my family now and you always will be so please come to me if you ever need anything."

I touched his hand gratefully, thankful for his kindness.

"Thankyou Cal, truly...but I am alright."

*   *   *

As I opened the door to my own house, I could smell burning candles.

Confused, I closed the door behind me and walked into the kitchen where the dining table was set up nicely with the silver cutlery, two wine glasses and two white candles burning slowly. I turned my attention to the vision of my husband, cooking at the stove, stirring something in a saucepan with a wooden spoon.

I was dumbfounded. Jacob never cooked. In the whole time we had been together, I think he had only ever cooked when I'd not been at home. Plus, I was very surprised to see him back from his golfing day already.

I dropped my keys onto the counter just inside the kitchen doorway, alerting him to my presence.

Jacob whirled around, his wooden spoon gripped tightly in his hands.

"Ellen! You're back!"

"Well yeah, I live here," I reminded him, confused as to what was going on. He snorted, briefly laughing at that.

"I know that! I saw your note that you'd gone to see Cal so I thought I would cook dinner for us. I was just hoping to be finished before you got back. Another five minutes or so would have been perfect," he told me, striding over to me and placing a kiss on my cheek.

I still wasn't understanding any of this.

"OK but I wasn't expecting you to be back from your golf day so soon either. I came back to cook dinner in time for when you got home so I'm a little confused as to why you're back so early and why you're cooking for us when you never normally do," I told him.

He smiled at me, stealing himself back over to the stove and giving his cooking another stir before he replied to me.

"I had a good think about last night and how I treated you...I realised that I was cruel to be like that with you when all you've ever done is love me and everyone around you. I think you're beautiful and I don't know why I said what I did last night so I can only apologise for that. So, I came home early and found you were gone which then I decided to cook dinner for us both in order to start trying to make amends. I've got everything planned out. First we'll have dinner, then we'll watch a movie and then, we'll continue with what we started last night. As long as you forgive me of course, but I'm hoping to show you just how much I love you and your body if you will allow me to."

I breathed in sharply. I couldn't recall the last time he'd tried to make amends with me or had even asked for me to forgive him. What on earth was going on? Should I just accept it? We were married after all and all couples had arguments. Here was my husband trying to apologise for how he'd been so maybe I should accept it and get over it. Maybe.

"Alright, that sounds like you've planned a nice evening for us," I acquiesced, "what can I do to help?"

"Nothing! You just take a seat there at the table for me. Dinner will be ready in a few minutes. Grab yourself a seat and I'll pour the wine," Jacob told me, grinning at me as he realised I was going to let him try and make things right again with us.

I made my way over to the table and sat down, alert to Jacob's every move as he grabbed a bottle of rose wine from out of the fridge and brought it over to me. He unscrewed the lid off of it slowly, pouring the wine into first my glass and then his own.

"Cheers," Jacob said, raising his glass and waiting for me to chink mine against his. I raised my glass and did as he wished before I took a sip. Mmmm, that was delicious. I had to give the man credit, he knew which my favourite wine was.

I continued to sip at my drink whilst I watched Jacob dish our dinner up. It looked (and smelt) like he'd made a curry for us. I couldn't say I was too surprised, he needed something to make that was easy to do. I didn't mind though, I was appreciative of the fact that he was making this effort to cook for me. He placed the plate of curry that he'd served up for me in front of me, then sat down at the table with his own plate and grinned at me.

"I hope you like it," Jacob told me, "it's been a while since I've made a curry but I know you like them so thought I'd give it a try. Go ahead, eat some and let me know what you think."

I picked up my fork and dug into the delicious smelling food on my plate and popped it into my mouth. Wow, it was really good!

"This is really tasty Jacob! Thankyou."

He smiled at that, starting on his own food now that he knew that I liked it. We sat in silence as we ate, appreciating the food and the company whilst the candles flickered between us from a small breeze. I was about halfway through when I decided that this would probably be the best time to tell Jacob that I'd applied for college.

"Jacob? Do you remember how I was saying I wanted to do a nursing degree and you agreed?" I began, studying his face to make sure that he was still in a decent mood. I wanted to stop if it became obvious he was going to get mad all of a sudden, but it would seem that luck was on my side for once.

"Yeah, it's a great idea babe. You'd be fantastic as

a nurse! Why do you ask?" he queried, pausing in his eating to take a gulp of his wine as his eyes remained on my face.

"Well, when you went out to play golf this morning, I decided to look into it properly and discovered that I need to have a certain qualification before I can apply for the nursing degree I want to do so I rang the local college up and applied for one of their night courses. I should get all of the information through shortly but from what the lady said on the phone, I've basically got a place on it. It will take a year to do roughly and then next year, I can go on to do my nursing degree as long as I pass this course."

Jacob froze at that, a panicked expression flitting across his features briefly before he visibly relaxed.

"You've applied? How are we paying for this?" he asked me casually, causing me to wonder why he'd had such an odd reaction visually.

I breathed in deeply to steady myself before I answered him.

"I'm paying for it out of the savings I've accumulated. We're comfortable here and I pay my share of the bills as you know so I thought I would treat myself out of my own money. I didn't expect you to pay for my education so I thought this would be the best idea. I hope that you agree?" I asked him, hoping that he would indeed agree with me without thinking I should have used the money on something for us. I didn't do much besides work so this was going to be something major for me but I also knew how Jacob's mind worked. He nearly always expected me to spend my money on something he thought we needed or for us to go out somewhere that he chose. This was about me for once and I was pleased that I'd been able to pay for it myself.

To my surprise, Jacob beamed a smile at me, reaching over to take my hand in his.

"Of course babe, if that's how you want to pay for it. I wouldn't have minded helping you though. This will be a great thing for you...plus it means that when you've passed your degree at university, I'll be married to a sexy nurse. Promise me you'll wear your nurse outfit for me sometimes?" he pleaded, his eyes twinkling dangerously as he gazed directly into my eyes.

I grinned shyly, a crimson blush creeping up my neck and along my cheeks.

"I guess I could do that," I replied huskily.

Jacob scraped his chair backwards and rose up, striding around to my side of the table and cupping my face in his hands to lift it up towards his mouth as it descended upon my lips. He kissed me deeply, brushing the loose strands of my hair away from my face until he pulled back, directing his eyes to bore into mine.

"Come with me," he muttered, taking me by the hand to lead me upstairs.

I followed him, butterflies fluttering around in my stomach even though they weren't fluttering in a good way. I was feeling nervous. After the comments he made the previous night, I wasn't sure how I was supposed to be in the bedroom now. Was he actually interested in me like that? I know he said and acted like he was, but he'd also said that he didn't find me as attractive as he used to so I was nervous about how this was going to go.

He led the way into the bedroom and I entered behind him filled with trepidation, keeping a careful eye on my husband as he turned back around to face me. His eyes slowly travelled down my body, taking me in with his gaze before his eyes travelled back up. He must have seen something in the expression on my face because he ambled over to me, lifting my chin with his fingers to look at him properly.

"What's wrong?" he whispered, stroking a thumb across my cheek tenderly.

"Are you sure you want me? I mean, are you still attracted to me?" I asked tentatively, lowering my gaze so that I could avoid seeing his response.

"Of course I do! I love you, Ellen! I know I said

Broken Tulips

some horrible things last night but I promise you, I didn't mean any of it! I'm not even sure why I said it, but to me you are the most beautiful woman in the world. You're kind, you're sexy and I'm a very lucky man to have you. Let me show you?" he asked quietly, trailing his fingers down my arm causing me to shiver at the touch. He knew that I loved it when he did that.

I nodded my acquiescence to his request, waiting to see what he would do. He pressed a gentle kiss to my lips, taking me by the shoulders and steering me over to the bed as he did so. He continued to kiss me as he swiftly raised my top up off and over my head, breaking his kiss momentarily before crashing his mouth back onto mine as his hands moved to my jeans and began to push them downwards.

I had to admit, I wasn't feeling the intimacy all that much but I obliged him, thinking that maybe it would get better as things progressed. I helped to shuck my jeans down my legs, stepping out of them as they landed on the floor and almost stumbled back as Jacob grabbed at my breasts that were encased in my bra, not unlatching his lips from my mouth as he did so.

I grunted at how hard he'd grabbed them, pushing him back slightly which made him pause and look at me in confusion.

"Can you ease up a bit Jacob? You're being a bit

rough," I grumbled, my desire still only burning as embers, waiting to be truly ignited.

He mumbled his apologies before rubbing my breasts gently whilst he lowered his head to my shoulder and feathered kisses there. I closed my eyes and arched my back into his hands, pushing my breasts further into his touch as he finally began to handle me as he should have the first time around.

When I eventually opened my eyes and looked back at him, I noticed his shirt and trousers had somehow disappeared. I wasn't sure when he'd gotten rid of them as I was pretty sure that his hands hadn't left my body. Before I could think further upon it, he tugged at my knickers hard, ripping them from me as the seams broke.

"Ouch!" I cried, the desire he'd begun to stoke within me firmly being doused by the pain that he'd just caused by removing my underwear in such an indelicate manner. I'd read about people doing things like that in books but it had always been portrayed as something romantic and urgent, whereas in this reality, it just plain hurt.

Jacob froze, his face panicked.

"I'm so sorry! Are you alright?" he babbled, crowding me as he got as close to me as possible.

"No! I'm not, that hurt! What is wrong with you lately?" I demanded, glaring at him as I climbed onto the bed and examined the back of my leg where the pain was. There was a bright red mark there from where my underwear had strained against my leg before breaking.

"Nothing is wrong with me babe! I was just excited and was trying to hurry things along," he muttered, sulking like a little schoolchild as he took a seat next to me on the bed. He moved his hand closer to me as though he were going to touch my shoulder but I flinched, turning my head away from him.

I couldn't help the disgust I felt by the idea of him touching me right then. I stood up abruptly, moving over to the chair that was placed near to the bed and picked up my nightdress that lay across the back of it. I pulled it on over my head quickly before returning to the bed and climbed into it, pulling the covers over me as I did so. I heard Jacob sigh behind me as I lay down, hugging the covers close to me.

"Is that it? We're done now?" Jacob asked, his displeasure plain to hear in his voice.

"Yes. We're done. First, you insult me as you did last night. Second, you hurt me whilst trying to hurry things up without attempting to make me feel desirable. What am I to you exactly? A wife to love and cherish as we promised in our vows? Or a piece of meat for you to pleasure yourself with when you feel like it without any concern for me during the process?" I questioned him, unable to hold my tongue. This argument had indeed been a long time coming.

I heard him scoff from where he sat at the end of the bed.

"What pleasure am I meant to be getting when I'm married to such an ugly, overweight disgusting woman who won't even let me make love to her?" he snarled at me, his vehemence coming through violently.

I sat up again and stared at him in hurt surprise.

"Is that what you think of me then? What you started to say last night is what you truly think?"

"Yes! No! I don't know," he whined, his head falling into his hands in obvious frustration, "you make me crazy Ellen! I love you but I don't know how I feel about you anymore! Since your sister died, you've changed! You're sad so much of the time and I understand you're upset by her passing but enough is enough! You're my wife and you should act like it! You used to go to the gym to keep your body in shape but you stopped going and I can see it."

I sat there in stunned silence then. Of course I'd changed when my sister had died, she'd been the last living relative that I'd had and I mourned for her. Had I been as upset and down as he claimed? If I had then I hadn't meant to be but if I couldn't be myself around my own husband then who could I be myself around? I didn't know what to say to him. Was this the end for us? I lifted my head, facing him directly.

"If you feel that way then what are we still doing together?" I asked him quietly, unable to see any way to resolve this tonight.

"Because I do still love you Ellen," he stated, his eyes gazing back at me in sorrow, "and I have loved you for years. You know I have. So I don't want to lose you but if we're going to be together, we're going to need to make some changes. We both are."

I sighed, unsure of what we should do.

"So, what now?"

"I'm going to go downstairs and sleep on the sofa tonight to give us both some time to ourselves and I think we should both think about what we want and let each other know in the morning," Jacob told me, "we need to both decide if our marriage is worth fighting for. Goodnight Ellen."

With that, he rose from the bed, pulled on his boxers and left the room, leaving me staring after him as I tried to comprehend what had just happened.

CHAPTER FOUR.

It was the next morning and I was feeling extremely anxious about going downstairs to see Jacob. I had done a lot of thinking the night before, going over absolutely everything in my mind before I decided on what I wanted to do.

I knew that Jacob had been out of order, that had been obvious, but I also realised that maybe what he'd said wasn't totally unfounded. I *had* stopped going to the gym before Amber passed away due to trying to be there which was of course understandable to Jacob, but maybe I'd let myself go too much. Plus, I hadn't had my hair done in months, I'd stopped wearing makeup and half of the time, I just wore my comfortable clothes because I'd lost interest in making an effort in myself. So perhaps if I started investing some time and effort into myself once again, then maybe Jacob and I might work.

Even though he had been a class A jerk, I didn't want to give up on our relationship just yet. I didn't want to have a failed marriage behind me simply because I'd made my husband feel unattracted to me. So I decided to head downstairs and see what Jacob wanted to do before we could move forwards, either together or apart. I just had

Broken Tulips

to go and find out.

I crept down the stairs, searching around me as I tried to locate Jacob. I found him sitting hunched over on the sofa, his head resting in his hands whilst his elbows rested on his knees. He wore a tank top along with his boxers this time around.

I cleared my throat as I neared him, alerting him to my presence and he whipped his head up, his eyes roving over my face as I approached him.

I sat down on the sofa with him albeit at the opposite end to him, not sure how to start this conversation. I glanced nervously over at him, hoping he would take the plunge to begin this. Luckily he did.

"Listen Ellen," he began, lowering his hands to rest on his knees, "what I said last night was out of order and I know it was...but we do have problems and we need to address them. Did you think about what I said? About having a think about what we both want from us?"

I nodded my head slowly, licking my lips to moisten them as they'd suddenly gone dry.

"Good. I will be honest with you, I don't want to give up on us. I want to see if we can try and get back to where we were if we can. I meant what I said, I do still love you and I care for you deeply but I've felt unwanted for quite some time. So I guess, the question is do you still want to be with me?" he asked me, his face drawn from the long night we'd both had the previous evening.

"Yeah. Yes, I do still want to be with you," I replied softly, twiddling my thumbs in my nervous state, "and I understand that you have probably felt unwanted but you do have to remember that it has been a very traumatic time recently which is why I've not been my usual self. However, I know that I've let myself go a bit and that's not what you signed up for when we got married so if we stay together, I promise to start going back to the gym and wear makeup and get my hair done again. I'll try my best to be the wife you married as long as you promise to be supportive of me if I'm having a bad day regarding the loss of Amber."

Jacob thought for a few moments before turning his gaze fully on me, a gleam in his eye as he gave me a small smile.

"I think I can do that," he replied finally, "I will support you babe, I hope that you do know that. Like I said, I was out of order with you last night but at the same time, I can't help feeling what I feel."

"I know," I acknowledged, "but what you said to me also has repercussions. I feel kind of insecure about my body right now so perhaps if we try going back to the dating stage of our relationship and try and get the spark back whilst I'm getting myself back into shape at the gym, maybe that could be a good idea? What do you think?"

His face broke out into a huge grin then as he nodded his head enthusiastically.

"Yeah I can agree with that! I'll make you feel sexy again and then, when you're ready, we'll consummate our relationship once more and behave as though it's our first time once more. I can see this being so much fun," Jacob told me, holding his hand out for mine.

I gave him a small tight smile as I let him take my hand in his and he rubbed my knuckles with his thumb soothingly.

We sat like that for a few minutes, neither one of us saying anything as I didn't know what to say but I also didn't know what he was currently thinking. Was he truly happy with the decision we had made? I guessed only time would tell. He breathed in sharply, alerting me to the fact that he wanted to speak again. I waited for him patiently until he spoke.

"I truly am sorry Ellen," he muttered, his eyes averted from my gaze as if he couldn't look at me, "I know it's my fault too and I really shouldn't have been like that with you. I'm sorry I hurt you too, that was never something I intended to do. I actually had thought it would be sexy."

He scoffed to himself, shaking his head at his own actions that had brought all of this on. I squeezed his hand gently.

"It's OK Jacob, I know you didn't mean to hurt me. I was angry last night and we both said things that we didn't mean. That's what people in relationships do though right? Have massive arguments and then make up? Well we're trying to work through it and that's the main thing isn't it?" I asked, trying to sound positive even though I didn't fully feel it yet.

"Yeah that's right! And we *will* get through this babe, I know we will," he told me before leaning forward to give me a kiss on the cheek.

He stood up abruptly then, letting me know he was going to get ready for work but that he was happy that we were trying to keep our marriage from falling apart. I smiled at him as he threw on his work clothes before heading out, calling goodbye to me as I watched him leave.

I slumped back against the sofa, the breath gone from me as I tried to figure out what I was going to do next.

I could hear Amber's voice in my mind, telling me that I was an idiot for staying with Jacob and for admitting that it was mostly my fault. I believed my conscience was trying to tell me that but I didn't know what to do. I'd been with Jacob for so long and I knew that if I did the things that I said I would do then things would probably go back to being really good between us. I just hoped that I would feel comfortable enough around him to be able to make love to him again and I hoped that I would be able to forgive him for the things that had transpired in the past few days.

I hoped.

*　　　　*　　　　*

Just over a month passed since my chat with Jacob.

Things were getting better although we hadn't taken things into the bedroom other than for sleep yet. I'd been going to the gym and luckily, my muscle tone memory activated rather quickly so I was already almost back to being the same figure as I used to be, slim and toned. I'd gone to the hairdressers and gotten my hair cut, I'd bought some new clothes that accentuated my figure and I'd begun to wear makeup once more.

I had to admit, I was starting to feel good about myself. Jacob had even complimented me a couple of times on my appearance which had made me blush so I knew I was starting to get somewhere with this overhaul on myself.

I'd seen Cal a few days before and he had commented on the fact that I was looking different. It hadn't taken him long to grind me down and tell him about what had occurred between Jacob and myself. Needless to say, he was furious with Jacob, unable to understand why I'd chosen to stay with him. I'd told him my reasons, although they'd sounded hollow but I really couldn't give up on my marriage. I'd always been taught to fight to keep your loved ones so that was what I was doing.

Cal had accepted what I'd said eventually but told me that if I ever was in need of somewhere to stay or escape to, then he'd always have room for me which I had to admit, had made me feel so welcome and loved.

I'd thanked him whilst spending time with Lily before returning home.

Now, it was time for my very first night class and I was super excited. We'd had an induction evening already so I'd already made a couple of friends but most of the students were younger than I was with only a mere handful of them being near to my own age. Ah, the joys of being in my mid-thirties and back in the learning environment.

I felt like a grandma.

The first class went great, my spirits high as I left and walked out with another woman and a couple of the men that were there. We laughed with each other as we shared a few jokes and as it was only half past nine, we all agreed to go to a pub for a quick drink.

As we sat and drank, I learned that the woman's name was Abbie whilst the two men were called James and Aaron and we all had a very similar sense in humour. I got along with them greatly, much to my delight and we all swapped numbers so that if we needed any help with any of our coursework then we would have someone to call. We also decided then and there that we would all arrange to meet up a few times throughout our educational journey and keep our newfound friendships going.

By the time I left them all and drove back home, I was in a good mood for the first time in quite a while. Things were looking up and I was gaining new friends for the first time in an age. It had been refreshing to spend time with others also trying to better themselves for the sake of a new career.

I hummed a merry tune as I walked through the front door of my house, striding into the kitchen where Jacob was pouring himself a beer from out of a can. He turned to face me with a smile tugging at the corners of his mouth before he raised the glass to take a swig of his drink.

"I take it your first night went well?" he asked, amusement lacing his tone.

I smiled back at him, nodding my head as I dumped my bag down on the kitchen table.

"Yes," I sang happily, "it was very informative although I won't lie, it was kind of boring! But I don't mind…I made some friends too."

Jacob came over to me, his beer in hand as he wrapped his arm around my waist and pressed a kiss to my cheek. He whispered in my ear,

"Are these the people you went for a drink with?"

"Yes. There was a really lovely lady there called Abbie whom I got along well with. We swapped numbers so that we can call each other if we get stuck with our coursework."

His hand squeezed my side gently as he spoke again.

"I'm glad you're making friends babe. You seem a lot happier tonight and I'm pleased to see it. You're also looking drop dead gorgeous by the way…how would you feel about us taking things to the next level?"

I paused, unsure of where he was going to go with this. The short time that we had been retracing our steps as a couple had been good but I'd known that he would want to begin taking up our matrimonial duties after a certain amount of time. He was a man after all, but I was still nervous.

I knew I'd gotten myself back to being 'desirable' in his eyes, even if I didn't feel it. It was now or never. We would be finished with each other if I refused him now.

"Of course babe," I replied slowly, "shall we take it upstairs like we did the very first time?"

Jacob grinned at me and took me by the hand, leading me up the stairs without another word.

CHAPTER FIVE.

A couple of months into my college course and the group of friends I had made organised a night out in London for us all.

My marriage with Jacob seemed to be getting better and although I invited him to go with us to London, he apologised and said he would stay at home so that I could have some fun with my newfound friends. Secretly, I was pleased that he wasn't going to go. Even though things had been going well between us, I still didn't feel fully at ease with him. I constantly felt as though I were walking on eggshells, afraid that I would do or say something that would bring about his nasty side once more. I thought to myself for the hundredth time that we should have never gotten married as young as we had.

We'd married a mere year after we first got together as we believed we were completely in love. The past several months had shown me that I still had much to learn about the husband I had spent so many years with.

The evening for the London trip came and I went to meet Abbie and the others at the train station, looking forward to having a night away from everything. Jacob dropped me off at the station, kissing me on the mouth before I vacated the car and left him. I promised him that I would get a taxi back home so that he could do as he wished with his evening without worrying about not being able to drink if he had to come and pick me up. He had agreed heartily, filling me with relief that I wouldn't need to worry about angering him if he were to wait for me.

"Yes! You're here!" Abbie squealed excitedly as I strode over to where her and the others were stood, waiting. I smiled warmly at her as she swung her arms around my neck in greeting in a friendly hug.

"Of course I am," I chuckled to her, smiling my greeting to everybody else. There was about six of us going and I had found that we all got along very well.

We'd all bought our tickets a few weeks previously so we got onto the train as soon as it arrived and we were on our merry way.

I stayed by Abbie's side for a while, feeling a bit uncertain of myself in this large group as it had been a long time since I'd gone out with friends. Luckily, my awkwardness was short lived and I was able to relax fairly swiftly, engaging animatedly in the conversations as we moved from place to place in the huge city.

We ambled into a crowded bar after a couple of

hours and I was starting to feel the effects of drinking too much wine. I offered to get the drinks in this bar whilst the others found somewhere to sit. I ordered our drinks at the bar, adding a glass of water to the list in the hopes that I could down it before joining the others at the table.

"Needing a glass of water already?" someone asked me as I took a big gulp from the glass that had been placed in front of me. I turned quickly, spilling some of the water down myself as I came face to face with Ryan, Cal's brother.

"Ryan?!" I gasped, pleased to see his friendly face on this fun evening out.

He grinned at me and leant towards me, pressing a swift kiss to my cheek in greeting before he spoke to me.

"What are you doing here?"

"I'm on a night out with my college buddies, how about you?" I asked him, unable to tamper the smile that had burst into life upon my face. He always seemed to make me feel at ease whenever I saw him.

"I've just come for a quiet drink. I got bored at home so decided to come out. Didn't expect to bump into you that's for sure!"

"I'll leave you to it then, I don't want to intrude your quiet drink," I told him, chuckling mischievously as I did so.

Ryan reached out and caught my arm as I went to turn away from him, the drinks in a tray in my hands as I stilled and cocked my head back towards him.

"You're not intruding at all. Do you think your friends would let me steal you for a drink for a quick catch up?"

"I don't see why not...but would you mind helping me with their drinks first? I bought the round so that I could sneak a glass of water without being called a lightweight," I informed him conspiratorially.

Ryan nodded his head then and took the tray of drinks from me, waiting for me to lead the way. I strode over to where my friends had sat down and introduced them to Ryan before excusing myself from them for a little while. I promised them I would be back soon but I wanted a quick catch up with Cal's brother. They'd all heard about Cal so they bade us to have fun as Ryan and I went back to the bar so that Ryan could order his drink. I held mine in my hand as Ryan studied me, his gaze travelling up and down my body before he spoke.

"You're looking good," he said, taking a swig of the beer that had just been placed in front of him. I blushed and glanced down at my feet, tucking a loose strand of hair behind my ear.

"Thanks," I muttered, "so are you."

"Ha, I just look as I always do," he replied, "but you've changed since I last saw you. Did you go back to the gym? Cal told me you were planning to?"

My smile faltered as I gazed at him then, narrowing my eyes as I wondered what else Cal had been telling his brother about me.

"Yes I did. I try and go at least three times a week if I can. What made Cal tell you something like that?"

Ryan gestured for us to find a booth to sit in so that we could have some more privacy. I followed him and sat down in a seat across from him before he answered me, his face solemn as he watched me.

"He told me about Jacob."

"And what did he tell you about Jacob?" I asked nonchalantly.

"He told me about what happened between you and Jacob a little while back and about how things appear to be now. He told me that even though things seem to be a bit better for you, he still doesn't think you're happy."

I sighed to myself, frowning before taking a gulp of my wine. I set my drink back down upon the table, not sure whether to be angry that Cal had betrayed my trust or to cry as I wanted to do now at the fact that Cal was right. I wasn't happy. Not at all. How awful did that sound?

"Can I ask, why was Cal telling you all of this Ryan?" I enquired, thinking to myself that was probably my safest option. I saw Ryan sigh as he ducked his head, picking up his beer and swigging from it.

"Honestly? I was asking after you and he seemed troubled by something. I pressed him until he told me," came the answer, "I'm sorry, I know it's none of our business but Cal is really worried about you even if he won't tell you...and if I'm honest, so am I. Why are you staying with this guy when he clearly isn't treating you very well?"

"He's treating me alright now. Things have been a lot better," I told him defensively.

"But that's only because you've changed to please him," Ryan pointed out, "so what if you'd stopped going to the gym? Yeah you look mega hot right now but you were sexy when you'd stopped going too."

That comment caught my attention.

"You thought I was sexy? Even when I'd stopped paying attention to myself and was looking pretty awful?"

I didn't believe him. He was obviously just being nice to me. Ryan scoffed at that, shaking his head in what I believed to be disbelief.

"Is that what your husband told you?" he asked me then, reaching across the table to take my hand in his, "you never looked awful, Ellen. You've had a very hard year what with losing Amber and dealing with your childish husband, but you never looked awful. You're beautiful always."

My breath caught in my throat. I didn't understand what was happening here. Since when had Ryan found me attractive? He *must* just be being kind to me.

"Thanks but you're just being nice. Me and Jacob are fine though so don't worry."

I raised my wine glass to my lips and took a deep gulp of it, feeling Ryan's eyes on me.

"I'm not just being nice, Ellen," Ryan murmured to me, "if you were single, I'd happily ask you out on a date. Unfortunately, you're married to Jacob so I'll just have to wait until you get fed up of him. Promise me one thing though, do not let him treat you badly again. If he does, go straight to Cal or call me to come and get you. We are always going to be there for you."

I blinked at that, the passion in his voice as he said those words surprising me immensely. I hadn't known he'd felt that way but then again, how would I have known? I'd never spent any time with him on our own. I nodded my head slowly, not breaking my gaze from his.

"Of course. If I need to, I'll leave," I told him, not saying a word about anything else that he'd just said. If I did, I knew that I would be playing with fire. I may have been unhappy with my husband, but I was definitely loyal.

*   *   *

I arrived back home several hours later, giggling in my drunken state as I fell through the door and shushed myself at the amount of noise I was making.

I giggled again loudly, forgetting instantly why I'd tried to shush myself. I paused as I thought about it. Oh yeah. Jacob.

I gazed about me to see if he was downstairs anywhere but I could not find him in the lower levels of our house. I shrugged my shoulders uncaring, feeling relieved that I didn't have to face him in this state. He must have been asleep in our bed upstairs which suited me fine. I just hoped that I wouldn't wake him when I too went to bed.

I stumbled over to the sink and after grabbing a cup, I poured myself some water and gulped it down, hoping to sober myself up enough to make it upstairs and into bed quietly.

Julie Thorpe

Once I'd drank that first cup, I poured myself another to be on the safe side. As I gulped the water down, I thought back to the fantastic evening I'd just had. Ryan had joined my friends with me after we'd had our chat, laughing and sharing stories with each other and it had truly been a wonderful evening. I found it hard to recall when I'd had so much fun previous to that.

I smiled to myself as I finished my water and set the cup down.

I raised my eyes up towards the ceiling, my shoulders slumping at the idea of having to go upstairs to bed to my sleeping husband.

Rolling the kinks out of my neck before I moved, I heaved a sigh and pushed myself up to stand properly and made the climb upstairs, my movements slightly easier to make as the water worked its magic in sobering me up just enough to get up the stairs without accident.

I reached the bedroom door and gently pushed it open, spotting my husband lying in the bed immediately. The only problem was that he was not alone.

There, in the bed next to him, lay a woman. The both of them were sound asleep but even in my inebriated state, I could clearly see that they were both naked. Their pale skin glinted in the moonlight that shone through the bedroom window, the limbs entwined with each other intimately.

I gaped in shock.

After everything that we had been through, was I really seeing this? My husband in bed with someone else? I shook my head, cursing out loud that I'd not seen it coming. Had I not been telling Ryan a few hours earlier that things were better? Had I not told him everything was fine now? How stupid I had been.

I closed my eyes and counted to ten, trying to calm myself down as the pain rolled through my heart. Jacob and the naked woman hadn't stirred when I'd gone into the room so after a moment, I crept back out of the room and went back downstairs carefully.

I wasn't going to make a scene tonight, no. I was going to confront him in the morning when I'd had a chance to sober up, even though I was starting to feel much more sober now after witnessing what I had seen.

I sank into one of the chairs at the table in the kitchen and placed my head in my hands whilst my elbows rested upon the table top. I wasn't going to cry, I refused to. My eyes were dry as my mind raced with what I should do next.

The clear thing to do was to leave him but I couldn't leave in the middle of the night without anywhere to go. I needed to speak to Cal as soon as

Julie Thorpe

he was awake...

CHAPTER SIX.

'Hi. I'm awake with Lily, what's up?'

Cal's text that I had been waiting for finally came through at 5am. I breathed a massive sigh of relief as I'd had visions of Jacob and his mistress waking up before I'd left and I didn't want to face him yet.

I was stone cold sober now as I had drank as many glasses of water as I could stand to drink and I'd also made myself a sandwich in order to speed up the sobering process. Thankfully, it had worked but now all I felt was the pain from discovering my husband in bed with another woman.

'I know it's super early but can I come over? I really need to get out of this house.'

Cal's reply came back within seconds.

'Of course you can.'

I smiled to myself. I knew that I could count on Cal to be there for me in my hour of need. I frowned as I looked at the time and realised I would have to walk to his being as I knew I still had alcohol in my system and couldn't drive.

'I'll be about half an hour. Got to walk, drank too much last night.'

I figured if I let him know how long I'd be, he wouldn't worry when I wasn't at his in five minutes time. Ping!

'Stay where you are. I'll come and fetch you. Give me ten minutes.'

I briefly considered arguing with him, but decided against it. I knew he wouldn't take no for an answer so I might as well accept graciously.

'OK. See you soon.'

I gazed about me, smoothing my clothes down as I checked myself in the mirror. I'd gotten changed into fresh clothes and wiped the makeup from off of my face so that I wouldn't look like a drunken mess when anyone saw me. I glanced at the note I'd left for Jacob on the kitchen table once more, making sure that he would be able to see it as soon as he came down the stairs. In the note, I had written that I had come home to find him with the woman in the bed and that I would be back to talk to him later on once I'd calmed down. I hadn't told him where I would be although I was sure that he would be able to guess.

Suddenly in the silence, I heard a bump come from upstairs.

"Shit!" I heard Jacob curse loudly as another bump came from above me and I knew that he had just woken up, probably trying to wake up the mystery woman to get rid of her before I came home.

Too late, I thought to myself. I saw car headlights appear outside of my house and I headed outside straight away, thankful that Cal had arrived when he had. I hurried over to the car, seeing Cal's worried face through the windows and I opened the passenger door and slipped inside, just as I saw Jacob open the front door of our house.

I stared at his shocked expression as he watched me drive away from him, before I turned around to face Cal.

"So....what's happened?" Cal asked softly, trying to watch me whilst keeping his eyes on the road.

"We're done," I stated.

What else was there to say? He'd cheated on me and there was no going back from that for me.

I heard Cal heave a sigh but he didn't say another word, simply driving us back to his in silence. I think he was waiting for me to tell him but I wanted to be safely in his house before I did. I didn't trust myself not to cry but I knew that I didn't want to.

Lily was gurgling away in her car seat in the back of the car and I turned about in my chair to smile and pull faces at her until we reached the house. I jumped out and grabbed Lily from out of her car seat whilst Cal turned the engine off and got out of the car himself. Cuddling Lily close to my body, I waited for Cal so that he could lead the way and unlock the front door. I followed him in, cooing at Lily to keep her entertained until we reached the living room.

I sat down in one of the seats and placed Lily on my lap, keeping her cuddled close to me as Cal took a seat opposite, waiting for me to speak.

"I'm sorry that you had to come and get me but I do appreciate it, so thankyou. I know it's really early to be dealing with drama."

I thought if I could try and lighten the mood then I would.

Cal frowned back at me, replying slowly,

"What kind of drama are we dealing with though? You've not told me anything other than you and Jacob are done. Want to tell me what's happened?"

I sighed, giving Lily my little finger to play with as I looked back at her dad, noting the concerned expression upon his face. Amber had chosen a good one in Cal, he was always there if you needed him.

"I went out last night with some friends from college," I began, trying to keep myself composed as I spoke, "I actually saw Ryan there! We went out in London you see. Well, I had a few too many so stayed out quite late because I was enjoying myself but when I came home, I walked in to my bedroom to find Jacob sleeping in our bed with another woman. They were both naked, I could tell that much and I didn't really know what to do so I waited for you to wake up and now, here I am."

Cal was quiet for a moment, taking in what I'd just told him.

"So, when Jacob saw us driving away when he opened the door...?"

"He'd only just woke up," I explained, "I left a note on the table for him to read but he woke up just as you pulled up outside so as ashamed as I am to admit it, I legged it out of there before I had to face him."

Cal nodded his head in a thoughtful motion.

"So you think he knows that you know?" he asked me.

"He will do by now, yeah. I told him in the note that I left that I'd walked in on him and seen what I'd seen. He can't deny it because why else would there be a naked woman in bed with him?"

I handed the baby in my arms back over to Cal then because she was starting to whimper, wanting her dad I felt certain. I was right, she stopped as soon as Cal was holding her within his arms again.

I smiled sadly at her, the hurt I was feeling washing over me once more as I struggled with myself not to cry.

I could see the pity in his eyes as Cal gazed back at me.

"I'm sorry to hear this Ellen. I know I haven't thought much to the way Jacob has been treating you recently but I never thought that he would cheat on you. I can only imagine how you must be feeling," he told me steadily, "if you want to stay here you know you're welcome to. Do you know what you're wanting to do?"

I shook my head unhappily, not sure about anything at that precise moment.

"Would it be ok if I crashed in the spare room to get some sleep for a couple of hours? I haven't had any sleep yet and I need to, even if it's just to sober me up."

"Sure, go ahead. Come back down whenever you're ready to," Cal gestured to the door, and I smiled gratefully at him.

I stood up and walked out of the living room, thankful I at least had somewhere to sleep so that I could clear my mind.

*   *   *

I awoke abruptly.

Looking about me, I took in the unfamiliar room and wondered where I was until the memories came flooding back. If I had had any doubts as to where I was, a pile of books in the corner of the room would have reminded me. Cal's spare room.

I groaned and rolled onto my back, remembering everything that had happened to make me be here. Bile rose in my throat as I thought about the fact that Jacob had had sex with a strange woman in our marital bed. Why had he done such a thing to me? We'd even been having sex again lately so it wasn't like I had denied him anything. I know things hadn't been right between us but I'd never thought he would do something like this to me. Never.

I sighed as I pushed myself up into a sitting position. Reaching down to the floor, I grabbed my clothes up from where I'd placed them after taking them off and pulled them on. Once I was dressed, I picked up my mobile phone to see what was awaiting for me.

Nine missed calls from Jacob. Twenty one text messages.

I rolled my eyes after reading the first message, skimming over the others briefly, all of them holding the same sort of message…sorry for hurting you, please come back, I love you. That sort of thing. I put the phone into my back pocket of my trousers and stood up. I supposed I'd better go and find Cal.

As I came out of the room I'd slept in, I could hear Cal's voice laughing and talking to Lily upstairs.

I glanced about me, locating the voice as coming from his study. I knocked on the door and stepped in when he called to me to enter.

Cal was sat at his desk working on his laptop whilst Lily sat in a walker, exploring the musical buttons on the walker and watching the lights that flashed all around it in glee if her smile was anything to go by. That vision made me smile too, happy that my sisters' family were doing alright.

Cal turned towards me, a small smile playing at the corners of his mouth.

"Feeling better after your sleep?" he asked, acting normal with me.

"Yes thanks," I replied warmly, "what are you working on?"

"Amber's story actually," Cal replied brightly, "I'm just finishing it. I'll probably be sending it over to Sally later."

"Wow, really?" I asked in amazement, "that's good going then! I thought it might take you longer to do."

Cal shook his head at me wryly.

"No, I didn't have to add too much but what I have written was hard to do so I've got to admit that I'll be glad when it's finished. But anyway, enough about that for now. How are you doing?"

"I'm alright I guess. To be honest, I just feel

hollow," I told him honestly. And that was how I felt. I felt empty, as though my emotions had drained away from me as I slept, leaving behind a hollow shell of a person to face the reality of the situation. "I hope you're morning has been alright though."

"Jacob came round a few hours ago, looking for you. I told him that you would see him or speak to him later when you were ready to, I hope you don't mind?" Cal queried, peering at me from under his lashes.

My stomach plummeted down to my feet at that news. Jacob had come here? I hadn't expected that. I'd been expecting him to be happy that he was free of me, regardless of the messages that he'd sent to me. When I realised that Cal was still waiting for me to answer him, I shook my head.

"No, I don't mind at all. Thankyou, I appreciate it and I'm sorry if it caused you any problems."

Cal waved his hand at me as if waving off my apology.

"Don't even worry about it," he told me, "you're family like I've said before and I'll always be here to help. It was fine anyway, if it makes you feel any better, he was looking very sorry for himself."

"He was?" I asked in surprise. Cal nodded his head in confirmation.

"Yup. I think he may be regretting what he's done."

I harrumphed at that and crossed my arms over my chest.

"Regretting he was caught more like. Alright, thankyou Cal. I guess I'd better go and face him then," I murmured, more to myself than to Cal but he heard me all the same.

Cal arose from his chair, stepped around Lily in her walker and strode over to me.

"Would you like me to take you back in the car?" he asked softly, hovering by my side as though he were uncertain of what to do. I supposed I couldn't blame him. This wasn't an easy situation to be involved in. I shook my head.

"Thanks Cal, but no. I'm going to walk back so that I have some time to figure out what I'm going to say to him. Thanks for helping me."

With that, I turned on my heel and headed out of the house and down the street, heading in the direction of my home where Jacob would be.

CHAPTER SEVEN.

I walked through the door to find a bouquet of flowers placed on the table, to be seen as soon as you walked through the door.

"Ellen?" I heard Jacob call from the living room. A moment later and he came into view, coming to an abrupt halt when he saw me stood by the door.

My heart was pounding, my palms were sweating. Oh God, I still hadn't figured out what to say to him whilst I'd walked here. My thoughts had churned the whole time so now I was still at a loss.

I saw Jacob hesitate whilst he decided what to do, until he stole over to me slowly, warily.

"Ellen? Can we talk?" he asked me then.

I breathed in deeply for strength before I replied to him.

"That's why I came back. We need to talk."

I stepped past him and into the living room, taking a seat upon the sofa whilst I waited for him to follow. I studied him as he came to sit down beside me on the sofa, noticing that he appeared quite pale, as though he were feeling sick. Good, I thought to myself.

"I'll let you go first. What did you want to say?" I asked him bluntly, fixing him directly in the eye with my gaze. He gulped.

"I know what you saw must have been pretty bad...but I promise, I never meant to hurt you."

I stared at him incredulously.

"Really? You didn't mean to hurt me? If that's true, why on earth did you sleep with someone else?!" I demanded, unable to believe my ears at the blatant lie that he'd just told me.

At least he had the good grace to look ashamed at my words. He hung his head, wringing his hands together as he took a minute before he replied.

"I don't know," he admitted, "you'd gone out with your friends so I thought I'd go to the pub and have a couple of drinks there instead of staying in by myself. The woman you saw, I met her at the pub. We got to talking and one thing led to another and she ended up back here. I'm so sorry Ellen, truly I am."

I narrowed my eyes at him and asked the question that had been bothering me ever since I received his first apology via text message.

"Are you sorry that you did it or sorry that you got caught?"

Jacob pursed his lips, the expression of guilt and shame deepening on his face. That was when I knew the honest truth. He was sorry that he'd gotten caught. At that horrid realisation, another ugly thought crossed my mind.

"Have you slept with someone else before this Jacob?"

He frowned, the guilt growing more and more upon his face as he closed his eyes so that he didn't have to look at me.

"Yes," he answered quietly, that one word punching a hole into my gut, "I need to be honest with you. Yes, I've slept with other people."

I sat in dumbfounded silence, unable to comprehend what he was saying. People? How many people had he slept with?

"How many others Jacob? And how long have you been cheating on me?" I demanded softly, my eyes glued to his face as I watched him squirm under my gaze. I felt oddly hollow and detached, as though I were watching everything happening from somewhere far away.

"I don't know how many, I've lost count," he muttered, avoiding my gaze, "and it's been happening for a few months now. I know that we have been getting on better and that you've done what you promised to do but I couldn't help myself. It was exciting, having these women come on to me and you never do that anymore. I thought you had gone off me."

I scoffed at that, unable to prevent it from escaping my mouth.

"You thought I'd gone off you? You know what? I have...but that is down to you being different with me. You've been distant, you've been cold and sometimes, you've been downright mean to me," I told him truthfully, deciding now was the best time to tell him how I felt, "yes, you've been better lately because we'd both promised to try to make our marriage work but we're flogging a dead horse aren't we? Our marriage is over and it has been for a while. We've just been too afraid to say it."

Jacob jerked his head up at that, shock replacing any other emotion on his features. He opened and closed his mouth a few times, coming across as though he were a fish.

"You can't mean that Ellen!" he eventually cried, reaching across to take my hand in his. I pulled my hand away before he could touch me, lacing the fingers on both of my hands together and placing them upon my knee. I didn't want him to touch me. Just the thought of it made me want to shudder in disgust.

"I do mean it," I said boldly, "I think we're both just staying together now because we've been together for so long and it's too daunting to be on our own. But you know something? I'm not afraid anymore Jacob. In fact, I think it would be the best thing for us now as I can't imagine touching you or kissing you or anything after seeing you in bed with that stranger last night. And now to know that she wasn't the first either, what's the point in us being together?"

Jacob shook his head frantically.

"No! Ellen, I know I've made mistakes but I still love you! I don't want you to leave me. I want us to grow old together! I want us to have a baby!"

What had he just said to me? A baby? What on earth made him think that we should have a baby? I couldn't even keep him faithful to me in our marital bed! I shook my head at him in disbelief, holding my hands up to my head as the beginnings of a headache were brewing.

"Did you actually just say that?" I commented, glaring at him now.

"Yes! We should have a baby! That's probably what we need to save our marriage," Jacob informed me, the serious expression on his face letting me know that he wasn't joking. I rolled my eyes at him.

"A baby won't save our marriage Jacob," I told him in a calm manner, realising that he wouldn't listen to hysterics when he was coming out with rubbish like that, "you being faithful was the only thing that would have saved our marriage. You broke your wedding vows to me and I'm sorry but this toxic relationship of ours is over. There's no going back. You must realise that we're no good for each other anymore? I'm not happy with you and you've made it clear on many occasions that you're not happy with me. Let's just call it a day shall we? You must see that I'm right?"

I hoped he could understand what I was saying. It was the only way forward for us. I'd always thought that I would be upset if Jacob and I were to ever split up but I wasn't. If anything, I felt as though a huge burden was beginning to lift from my shoulders.

I watched as the struggle took place on his face, trying to find a reason for us to remain together but slowly, surely, struggling to find one. He sighed after a few minutes, alerting me to the fact that he was giving in.

"You're right," he murmured, his shoulders slumping as he admitted it to me, "we would be better off apart…but I do still love you Ellen. Please know that I truly never meant to hurt you."

I took a hold of his hand then, squeezing it reassuringly.

"I know Jacob. I think you love me but you're not *in* love with me. And it's okay because I think I'm the same. We've tried to make our marriage work and it hasn't but we can at least say that we've tried. The fact that I'm not more upset than I am to know that you've been sleeping with other women kind of says it all doesn't it?" I asked him, hoping that I was helping him to realise that what I said was true.

He nodded his head.

"Yeah, good point," he agreed, glancing back up at me, "so what do we do now?"

I thought this over for a minute or two, trying to decide what would be the best course of action. I knew Cal would help me, he'd already said as much so I made a decision.

"I'm going to go and stay at Cal's. He has offered me the spare bedroom if I need it so I think I'll move out and stay there until I can find somewhere more permanent, as long as Cal is happy with that of course. You can keep the house, it's yours after all."

Jacob seemed surprised at my answer.

"No, it's our house," he stated slowly.

"No, it's your house Jacob. You already lived here and I moved in with you remember? It's always been yours."

I stood up from my seat then and told him I was going to go and pack some of my things up. I needed to call Cal and check that he was still alright with me staying in his spare room for the time being.

*   *   *

I'd called Cal and explained what was happening.

He had agreed in an instant that I could stay in his spare bedroom until I was able to find somewhere, no matter how long that took as he informed me. I was glad for that as I was feeling a bit lost.

I had just finished packing up some clothes into suitcases and shoving various bits and pieces of mine that I wanted into bags when Cal arrived to pick me up and take me back to his.

Jacob knocked on the bedroom door as I picked up some of my things and came over to me, his face solemn.

"Can I help you take anything down to the car?" he asked me gently, obviously unsure what else to say to me.

I nodded my head, gesturing towards a couple of bags that lay on the floor at my feet. If he grabbed those for me, then I would only have to do the one trip to the car with everything.

He leaned over and picked the bags up before following me down the stairs and out to Cal's waiting car. I placed my suitcases in the boot whilst Jacob put the bags that he was carrying onto the backseat of the car. Cal and Jacob exchanged formal greetings and then I turned back to Jacob, a lump forming in my throat.

This was all very real now and I was feeling sad at the end of this chapter of my life. I had spent a good many years of my life with this man so leaving him was quite difficult, even though we both knew it was the right thing to do.

Jacob looked down at his feet, scuffing his shoes against the curb.

"I'll be back for the rest of my stuff soon, Jacob. I'll obviously let you know when so that you're here when I come. Here's your keys," I said, handing over my door key for the house that we had both shared.

Jacob's face overshadowed with sadness, taking the keys from my outstretched hand.

"I'm so sorry for all of this Ellen," he muttered, repeating the apology that was already getting old to my ears.

I sighed, giving him a small tight smile.

"I know you are Jacob. But it turned out to be a good thing in the end. It helped us to realise that we're not suited for each other anymore. Like I said, I'll be in touch when I come to collect the rest of my stuff. Take care of yourself Jacob," and with that, I slid into the car that waited for me, indicating to Cal that we should go.

Julie Thorpe

He drove off, not saying a word as we headed back to his house, this time with a feeling of lightness in my soul as I began my new adventure of life without my husband.

CHAPTER EIGHT.

I moved into the spare room at Cal's house, only unpacking what I needed and anything else, I could grab from my bags as and when I might want them.

That first day was hard but I also felt unburdened so I knew in my heart that I had made the right decision. Cal had allowed me time to get situated in the bedroom, putting my clothes where I wanted them whilst he waited downstairs with Lily, prepping a nice Sunday roast dinner for us. He had already informed me that Ryan was coming around for dinner too but checked with me first that I was alright with that. I assured him that that was fine.

In all honesty, I wanted to thank Ryan for listening to me last night and obviously then tell him what had consequently happened since arriving back home. From what he'd said to me in the bar, I had the inclination that he might be happy at the news. Not that I wanted to be with anyone else just yet, but it was nice to know that men still found me desirable, even though my husband hadn't.

Once I was sorted in my new bedroom, I strolled down the stairs so that I could go and find Cal. He was sitting cross-legged on the floor whilst Lily was laying on her stomach on a multi-coloured blanket with various toys, hard and soft, dotted about her within arms' reach. She was giggling at the toy that Cal was currently pressing the buttons on which made different sounds, apparently finding it hilarious.

I smiled at the scene before me, glad that I had such a lovely place to come to in my hour of need. These two were my family and I couldn't imagine them not being in it. They were permanent fixtures in my life and I hoped that would never change.

Cal glanced up as I shifted my position slightly, straightening his back as he gestured for me to go in and sit down.

"Come in Ellen! Come and join us," he called to me.

How could I refuse such an offer? My smile widened as I strode over to them both, coming to a stop and kneeling on the ground.

"She's beautiful Cal," I breathed, unable to take my eyes off of my little niece.

"Yeah she is," he replied, the pride evident in his voice, "I love making her laugh. It lightens everything in my day."

I glanced over at him, watching as he pushed a small black and white book towards Lily, occupying her whilst he turned his attention to me.

"How are you holding up?"

"I'm doing alright. Don't get me wrong, I'm sad that it's happened and I'm sure I'll be more upset as time goes on and it sinks in more, but for now I'm doing alright. I actually think it was the best choice for us both," I replied honestly.

I knew I probably seemed quite cold hearted at that moment in time but it was how I was dealing with my situation. Cal seemed to understand however as he patted me on the shoulder in a comforting manner.

"I'm afraid I have to agree with you. If you need to cry or anything, feel free to go ahead. Don't feel like you can't just because you're here."

I gave a small chuckle at that, glancing back at Lily as she played with a teddy bear. It seemed she'd gotten bored of her book already.

"Thanks but I doubt I'll cry in front of anyone. I wouldn't want to scare your little girl here now would I? I've got to admit though Cal, I'm happy that I'm not at work today. I don't think that I would have been able to handle being nice to everyone all day long," I said, chuckling as I thought about how that would have gone down if I'd been at work. Badly, I was sure of it. At least here, in this house, I felt like I was home amongst people who cared about me.

"No, I doubt you could have," he agreed, chuckling

along with me, "I can imagine it must be very hard to work in customer service when you're dealing with problems such as these. At least in my line of work, I can hide out in my study away from everyone, but for you, you've got to be nice all of the time even when you don't feel like it."

I rolled my eyes mischievously.

"Yep and it's *hard*. Some of the customers we get in can be absolutely awful but you still have to stand there and smile, being all polite to them even when they're blaming you for how their steak is cooked wrong or how their salad isn't cold enough and all of that noise. I mean, how is it my fault how their steak is cooked? I just serve people on the bar! I don't cook their food!"

Cal started laughing at me, at my little tirade against ungrateful customers who came into my life on a daily basis. I couldn't explain how happy I was that I only worked Monday to Friday, considering I worked in a restaurant where almost all of the staff had to work weekends. There'd been a few grumbles from my colleagues of course, but I'd asked for weekday work and that was what had been agreed in my contract. I would do some weekends if they were expecting to be really busy or if someone called in sick, but that was it.

When I was younger, I would perhaps have worked as many hours as I possibly could but the older I'd gotten, the more I realised that I needed to look after myself too. So, I tended to do the day shift until six in the evenings during the week and that was it which suited me just fine.

"Sorry, I know that probably sounded mean," I apologised with a small smile.

"No, it's fine!" Cal replied swiftly, "it's funny to hear. You don't talk about work all that much so it's good to hear about it. How are the night classes going by the way?"

"Yeah they're great thanks Cal! I'm learning what I need to and the friends I've made are brilliant! Plus, if I hadn't gone out with them last night, I wouldn't have found out about Jacob now would I?" I asked breezily, belying the hurt that rose up within me.

Cal gave me a look at that but didn't say anything.

For the next couple of hours, we finished getting the dinner ready to cook then put everything on to cook through when the time was right and I played with Lily so that Cal could carry on with some bits around the house that he needed to get done. He joked that he'd be able to stay on top of things with me around to help but even though he was joking, I knew that he was being serious. I didn't mind helping him, if anything, I would be happy to help either with babysitting or with cleaning. This way, I could fulfil my promise to Amber that I would help to take care of her little family.

Dinner had almost cooked when the doorbell rang.

I ran to get it as Cal was changing Lily's nappy, opening the door to a warm smiling face. Ryan. He stared at me for a second before collecting himself and speaking.

"Hi! Erm…I mean this in the nicest way, but what are you doing here?" he asked me uncertainly.

I giggled, feeling slightly flustered.

"I'm guessing Cal forgot to let you know I would be here," I began, "I hope you don't mind?"

"No, not at all," Ryan replied quickly, panic shooting across his face, "I didn't mean anything by it. I'm glad you're here! It's just that you normally spend your weekends with Jacob so I was surprised to see you. That being said, is everything alright?"

The smile on my face felt frozen, so instead of answering him, I moved aside and gestured for him to come in. Thankfully Cal had finished with Lily by then, calling out to Ryan to head into the living room as he was just in time for dinner.

Ryan peered at me from the corner of his eye as he stepped past me but didn't say anything else. I shut the door behind him, sighing to myself. Why did it feel so hard to tell him that Jacob and I had split up? Maybe it was the fact that I had a failed marriage behind me and the fact that even though I knew there were men out there interested in me, I actually did feel as though I wasn't good enough thanks to my no good husband.

We all settled down at the table to eat whilst Cal served our dinner onto plates before bringing them out to us. I tried to help him but he insisted that I sit down and relax, talk to Ryan and look after Lily for him. I did as he said, keeping the conversation between Ryan and myself light, avoiding his gaze whenever he looked at me.

He must have known that something was off but he had the good grace not to say anything. Yet. Once Cal had put our dinners down in front of us, we all got stuck in and ate the lovely food he'd cooked for us all.

"Mmm, thanks for this Cal. You can't beat a good roast dinner," I told him, savouring my food.

He smiled back at me, finishing up a mouthful of potatoes before he answered me.

"You're welcome! Have you told Ryan your news yet?"

I gulped down the piece of chicken that I'd been chewing as the question startled me. I threw a glance in Ryan's direction, noticing that he had stiffened in his chair and was watching me, waiting for me to speak.

I cleared my throat noisily.

"No, I haven't yet Cal but now that you bring it up, I guess this would be as good a time as any," I shifted in my seat so that I faced Ryan properly, "Jacob and I broke up."

Ryan dropped his knife, the clattering sound when it hit the plate seeming quite loud. He stared at me.

"What?" he sputtered finally, "but you were only saying last night how things were getting better!"

"Yes, I did say that but it turned out I was wrong. There was another woman in my bed when I got home. Needless to say, Jacob and I have agreed that being apart from each other is probably the best thing all around so as of today, I'm single."

Ryan gaped at me, the shock on his face plain for me to see. Was it really so surprising to him after everything that he'd said? I squirmed in my seat, starting to feel uncomfortable at his staring, praying silently to myself that he would stop soon. I noticed then, that a small smile was tugging at the corners of his mouth.

"You actually left him?" he asked me, the smile beginning to grow wider.

I nodded my head slowly, not sure what was bringing about this strange reaction from him.

"Yes! Finally! Good on you Ellen! I'm so proud of

you for standing up to him!" Ryan cried out, his face beaming with his smile now.

I chuckled as I realised he was happy with the news after all. I ducked my head in embarrassment as Ryan whooped in his seat across from me. I could hear Cal laughing to the side of me.

"I'm guessing you're happy then Ryan?" Cal asked his brother, pretending that he hadn't noticed the reaction from his brother.

Ryan grinned at the both of us.

"Yes I am! I'm not going to pretend that I'm not because that would be an utter lie. Never liked the bloke and you deserve so much better Ellen," he informed me, leaning forwards in his seat as he began to talk more, "so now that it's officially over, what's your plans?"

I laughed at that. Plans? How did I know? We'd only just split up that morning!

"Ryan, I have no idea what my plans are. It only happened this morning. I'll have to find somewhere new to live that's for sure. Other than that, most things will stay the same probably," I shrugged, "work and college is the same as ever and other than my love life and home address changing, there's not much else to do."

Ryan mulled this over for several minutes, allowing us to continue eating as we waited for him to speak again. Knowing Ryan, he wasn't finished so it was best to simply wait for him to carry on.

It didn't take him long.

"I've got an idea," he began, turning his attention back to me, "why don't you book a week off from work and come and stay at mine for a holiday? I can show you around London! You've not been there much have you?"

"Ummm…" I started, not sure what to say. Was he just being nice or was he asking me out? He'd told me he wanted to last night so this could be a bad scenario. He must have realised what I was thinking because he held up his hands in a placating manner, smiling as he spoke again,

"Just as friends, I mean. You probably need a break to clear your head and London is great for keeping you busy! I thought it might help you move on if you were doing something fun?"

I relaxed at that, grateful that it wasn't some cheesy chat up line he was trying to get me back to his house. I thought about it, listening to Cal's encouragement from the side of me before I caved in and agreed. I let Ryan know that half term was coming up at college in a couple of weeks so I would ask for time off at work.

It would be nice to get away. I'd never seen London properly so with Ryan as my tour guide, I was sure I would have a good time.

CHAPTER NINE.

I stepped off of the train at the station in London Euston, searching about me for Ryan who ought to be waiting for me.

I spotted him in the main foyer stood next to the chocolate shop I loved. Hotel Chocolat. A friend of mine had introduced me to that shop a couple of years previously and whenever I saw one, I found myself going in to see what they had every single time. I couldn't help myself.

Ryan grinned at me as I hurried over to him, his hands held behind his back in a leisurely manner. I plastered a smile on my face in greeting.

"Hi! I made it," I breathlessly told him, feeling like I'd ran a marathon since I'd exited the train car. I hadn't of course, but the pace of the passengers disembarking from the train around me had spurred me to walk faster in order to keep up with everyone else. I must be a slow walker, I'd thought to myself as I'd hurried along with them.

He shifted his position, wrapping his left arm around me in a quick hug as he greeted me back.

"Yes, you did," he chuckled, bringing his other hand around to his front, a bag from the chocolate shop in his hand, "this is for you. If you're going to have a holiday then you should start it right."

He held the bag out to me which I took, taking a peek inside excitedly to find a large box of truffles inside. I glanced back up at him, a grin on my own face as I thanked him for the gift.

"How did you know I like this shop?" I asked in curiosity.

"Amber told me once. I'm not sure how we started on the conversation but she told me about how you always like to get something from this chain of chocolate shops so as there's a store in this station, I thought I'd get you a welcome gift. You do like truffles don't you?" he asked, his voice suddenly uncertain.

"Yes I love truffles," I reassured him as he leant forwards to pick my suitcase up from out of my hand, "you don't have to carry that Ryan! I can take it."

Ryan shook his head, taking me by the arm to start steering me out of the train station.

"I know you can but I'm being a gentleman. Or at least I'm trying to be," he winked at me as we ran down the steps that led into the station and hailed a taxi. Ryan explained to me that it would be easier to get a taxi back to his flat from there so that I could put my suitcase away before we decided what to do.

Ryan had called me a couple of days before I travelled to London to let me know that he was taking the time off from his job as a holiday too so that he could show me around his favourite city. When I'd told him I would have been fine, he admitted to me that he had been worried about me since my break up with Jacob, resulting in me agreeing to have him show me around. Thinking back on it, I'd realised it had been a very sweet thing for him to do.

It didn't take long for us to reach his flat and I followed him in as he stepped inside. I looked about me, studying his bachelor pad and scoffed.

"What?" Ryan asked me in surprise, turning to face me as he placed my suitcase on the floor.

"Oh nothing," I replied, trying to suppress the smile playing at my lips, "it's just that your flat is like the typical bachelor pad. I mean, seriously."

I gestured around me at the brown and grey colours that adorned his walls and made up the shades of his furniture, the pool table he had on the far side of the room, the gigantic television hanging on the wall with a unit below that housed his video game consoles. Everywhere I looked, the masculinity in the place was plain to see.

I chuckled at the sight. It was refreshing to be somewhere that was so different to what I had been used to.

I noticed Ryan frowning at me, apparently uncertain what to make of me.

"Um, is that a bad thing? It sounds like it would be a bad thing but your face looks happy. I'm confused."

"It's nice," I informed him, turning my gaze back to him, "it completes the feeling of being on holiday."

I saw that he was studying me, confusion apparent on his face but he didn't say anything else.

He showed me to the room that I would be staying in whilst I was there and once I was ready to head out, he asked me where I should like to go first. I contemplated my answer momentarily, pretending to think about it although I already knew where I wanted to go.

"Can we go to Madame Tussauds? I don't know how expensive it is but I've always wanted to visit it," I asked excitedly, unable to hide my joy at the idea.

"Don't worry about that. Madame Tussauds it is!" he exclaimed, clapping his hands together and leading me out of the flat purposefully. We took the Tube on the London Underground to get to the famous wax exhibition to be greeted by a shorter queue than I'd thought there would be. Phew! No standing around for hours to get in luckily!

In half an hour, we were in!

I was feeling utterly exhilarated at the fact we were at one of the places I'd always wanted to visit. Ryan laughed at me as I strolled around in childlike wonder, taking pictures of all of my favourite celebrity wax figures, sometimes with Ryan taking a picture of me standing next to them.

There was so much to see and the work was truly phenomenal! It took us a couple of hours to go around it all, chatting and laughing as we did so as we made jokes and talked about things we'd heard about various celebrities as we came across their wax form.

Hours later, when we finally made it back outside, I felt as though I was walking on air.

"That was amazing! Thanks Ryan," I enthused, turning my beaming face towards him, noticing that he was grinning back at me. As he continued to stare, I frowned a little.

"What?"

"I've not seen you this happy in months," Ryan replied gently, "it's nice to see."

My heart warmed at that comment.

"Well, I've not been happy for months. So thank-*you* for bringing me here. After everything that's happened this year, a fun holiday was just what I needed."

Ryan placed his arm around my shoulders as we

began sauntering down the street, searching for somewhere to eat as we were both hungry.

"You've had a lot to deal with but I've got to admit, you seem to be holding up better than I thought you might. There's fighter spirit in you," Ryan joked, poking me in the arm playfully, "have you heard anything from Jacob since we last spoke about it?"

I nodded my head thoughtfully, thinking back to the last time I'd spoken to my husband.

"Yeah I have. I told him I wanted a divorce and I've got a solicitor sorting out the paperwork for me so I'm definitely moving on with my life, saying goodbye to all of that," I replied, keeping my gaze steadily in front of me.

Ryan pulled me to a stop, forcing me to turn my gaze back to him.

"You filed for divorce?"

"Yeah. I can't stay married to the man if we're separated can I?"

Ryan shoved a hand through his hair, drawing my eyes to his neat, styled hair. *I wonder what his hair would look like if I ran my fingers through it and roughed it up a bit?* I wondered to myself. My face reddened as I realised what I was thinking. Where had that come from?

I shook my head slightly as Ryan began speaking

again, taking my attention away from his hair.

"That's true," he agreed, "but I thought it might take you longer to set things into motion. You've changed quite a lot in the past couple of weeks since you and Jacob split. You appear...freer than I've ever seen you."

"That can only be a good thing surely?" I asked him, uncertain of where this was going.

"Of course it is!" Ryan replied hastily, "I didn't mean anything bad by it. I'm glad you're happier, Ellen. Now, I don't know about you but I just want to go home and chill out. Shall we order a takeaway tonight and just relax? We've got all week for me to show you around."

I nodded my head after a moment, agreeing to his suggestion before we headed back to his place.

When we arrived back at the flat, we played some pool for a while as we waited for our takeaway to arrive. We'd chosen to have pizza this evening and when it arrived, we gave up on the pool to sit and watch a film on the television as we ate the pizza. That first night together was fun, we laughed, ate and spent time together in contentment as we grew to know each other a little more than we had before.

As I lay in bed that night thinking about it, we had never truly spent a lot of time alone together. Yes, we'd spent some time alone in the past but not much. Not enough to get to know each other. I liked Ryan, his demeanour so much like his brothers that I knew we were going to have a great time during this week we had together.

I was pleased, I needed a friend. Since Jacob and I had broken up, I had felt a new strength within me that I hadn't realised was there but I'd also felt a new loneliness that had not been there before. I'd felt a kind of loneliness whilst I was with my husband and now, I understood the emptiness of being truly alone at last. It bothered me, knowing that I hadn't been enough to keep Jacob content and so I wondered daily if there was something more that I could have done or if I was even unlovable at times, but then I would shake it off, remembering that what was done was done and had been the best decision for us all.

*   *   *

The next few days were spent visiting some of London's great landmarks. We went to Buckingham Palace in the hopes of seeing royalty (we didn't) but we saw the soldiers that stood guard outside of the palace, unmoving but ever watchful. It was a beautiful sight to behold, giving it much more justice than what it did when I'd seen it on the television.

Another day, we visited the London Eye, although

it was pouring down with rain so we didn't bother going on it as we knew there wouldn't be much to see. Instead, we went onto the Tower of London. When Ryan asked me why I wanted to go there on such a miserable day, I politely informed him that it would give the visitation a more authentic feel.

"It is a place of death, Ryan, but I want to go and see it because of the rich history that is there. In honour of the souls that died there, a rainy day will do nicely because if we went on a sunny day, it would just feel wrong," I explained to him.

He appeared to understand so we went there, taking a tour around the buildings and the grounds, listening to the gruesome history that had taken place there. It was thrilling and when we went into the gift shop at the end, I bought several books about the Tower of London so that I could learn more of the history. I couldn't explain why it excited me so much, but I'd always had a fascination with history and consequent historical places.

We spent several hours there before we retired for the day.

The next day, Ryan and I went to watch a show in the West End. It was a gift and a surprise from him to me. When he presented me with the tickets, I stared at him in shock.

"You bought us tickets? For the Phantom of the

Opera?" I gasped, taking them tentatively into my hands.

"Yes," came the quiet reply, forcing me to glance up at him in concern.

"What is wrong?" I asked him softly.

"Nothing, Ellen. I'm just pleased you like them. You do like them, right?" he questioned me.

"Yes, of course! This is my favourite play of all time but I've never seen it in the West End! Did you know it was my favourite?"

I studied him as a small wicked smile stretched across his face. He tapped a finger against the side of his nose, indicating that it was a secret. I laughed at that, swatting my hand against his arm and demanding that he tell me if he knew.

"Yes, I knew. Cal told me," he explained, "I called him up a couple of days ago to see if he could tell me what sort of plays you might like and he told me that you'd watched the film version of The Phantom of the Opera a few times and that you'd told him you wanted to see it live. So, here you are."

I was gobsmacked.

Ryan had gone out of his way to choose a show that I would want to see and kept it as a surprise for me. How thoughtful was this man? I gazed at him in wonder, discovering that he was able to surprise me over and over and I found that I liked it.

"Thankyou," I whispered, not knowing what else I could say that showed him how much this had meant to me.

His ears turned pink as he smiled shyly at me, informing me that we needed to get going if we were to make the matinee performance that he had chosen.

We arrived at the theatre without problem, finding our seats and settling in for a grand performance. The whole time that the show was being played out before us, I could feel Ryan's eyes on me at several points, causing me to feel warm and a little uncomfortable. Why was he watching me and not the show? Why did it make me feel as uncomfortable as it did? I already knew the answer. I was attracted to him and with him constantly throwing his gaze my way, I began to wonder if he was trying to make it obvious that he was checking me out.

As the play ended, I clapped my enthusiasm at having watched such an amazing show. Ryan leaned into me, his lips pressing close to my ear.

"I take it you enjoyed it?" he muttered to me, his warm breath whispering against my skin, causing me to shudder. He must have noticed because I heard him give a slight chuckle before he muttered into my ear again, making sure that I could hear him against the noise of the now departing crowd,

"Shall we go out for dinner tonight? I know a restaurant near to here that does decent food."

I agreed, standing up so that we could leave. We made our way out of the theatre, heading in the direction that Ryan led us in. We had been strolling along for about ten minutes when I wondered out loud how much further it would be. Ryan replied that it wouldn't be too much longer and fair to what he said, he pulled me to the side as we came to an Italian restaurant.

"We're here," Ryan muttered, then he placed his hand at the small of my back to guide me into the restaurant.

We were seated almost immediately once we were inside so as we took our seats, I gazed around me to see what it was like. There were small tables dotted all along the walls whilst large round tables resided in the middle of the room. The colour scheme for the restaurant was red and white whilst the lights were dimmed, giving it a cosy, romantic atmosphere.

I glanced back at Ryan, seeing that he was studying me.

"What?" I asked nervously.

"I was just watching your reaction to the restaurant. Do you like it?"

I smiled at him warmly before replying,

"Yes, it's nice. It's…cosy."

Ryan chuckled, looking down as he picked up two menus from the middle of the table and handed me one before opening his own to read.

"I thought you might like it," he murmured, not raising his eyes to me.

I narrowed my eyes at that. I wasn't sure what was going on here but I'd had a great day so far and I didn't want to ruin it by questioning him about it so I decided to read my own menu and choose something.

When the waitress returned to take our orders, I requested a lasagne whilst Ryan ordered spaghetti and meatballs.

We continued chatting whilst we waited for our food to arrive and then we quieted down a little when it arrived at the table, causing us to concentrate more on our food than our conversation. A couple of hours later, after eating some delicious dessert, we made our way back to the flat.

Ryan held the door open for me, allowing me to walk through first before he followed, closing and locking the door behind us.

"Thank you for today Ryan," I gushed in my joy at

such a fantastic day, "it's been amazing! I still can't believe you called up Cal just to find out what I would like to watch at the theatre!"

Ryan ambled over to me, taking a hold of my left hand in his own.

"Really? Of course I wanted to know what you would like to see. I'm here to help you have a good time and cheer you up remember?"

I glanced nervously down at my hand that was now encased in his.

"Erm, Ryan? What are you doing?"

"This," came his husky reply as he leaned down, dipping his head until his mouth covered mine...

CHAPTER TEN.

I stood, frozen to the spot as his lips descended upon mine.

After a few seconds, Ryan pulled back, a frown marring his face.

"What's wrong?" he asked me, uncertainty forming upon his features. Before I changed my mind, I grabbed the front of his shirt and yanked him back down to me, crashing my lips against his anxiously.

It only took a moment for his lips to begin moving, apparently getting over the shock of my reciprocation swiftly. He kissed me tenderly as his hands moved up my shoulders to entangle themselves in my hair.

I slowly relaxed, giving myself over to his kiss which felt strange after only having kissed Jacob for years. Strange, but nice.

His lips were soft on mine, persistent in their tasting of me as I stretched my arms up and around his neck, urging him closer to me.

I felt his tongue lick against the seam of my mouth, silently seeking permission to enter my mouth for exploration so I acquiesced, opening my mouth for his tongue to begin exploring. I'd always thought Jacob to be a good kisser but Ryan was better. Much better. His lips were soft and gentle upon mine, his tongue tentative as it explored my mouth, tousling with my own tongue as we tasted each other for the first time.

I'd always been told that you could tell how a man felt about you from his kisses and I was beginning to think it was true. The emotion behind this kiss I was sharing with Ryan was palpable, his care and attention undoubted as he caressed me with his lips.

He deepened the kiss, pressing harder against my mouth as the passion inside me began to rise up. Had I not only been wondering about running my hands through his hair recently? I reached up then and did just that, tugging on the strands of his hair blindly as my eyes closed involuntarily against the onslaught of emotions that were rising within me.

I'd known I was attracted to Ryan but I had never thought that we would do anything like this. I hadn't realised just how much I was attracted to him until he'd kissed me. Now, all I wanted was him.

I heard him moan against my mouth as my fingers tugged at his hair, feeling his hands sliding down my arms to caress my sides. I kissed him back harder, feeling the passion rising in him as well as myself.

Ryan moved me backwards, not breaking the kiss until I bumped up against the door. He held me there, lifting my arms above my head as he continued to lavish my mouth with his attention, a small groan escaping his lips as my leg accidentally brushed against his centre, feeling his excitement through his trousers with ease.

"I want you," he breathed against my lips, releasing them in order to trail kisses down my neck and along my collarbone. I arched into him, unable to speak as the desire coursed through me. I held onto his shoulders, grabbing tightly and holding him firmly against me.

I felt his hands moving, tugging at the hem of my top before he raised it up, peeling it off and over my head. I sucked in a sharp breath as I realised I was suddenly exposed to a man who'd never seen me in this way before.

I breathed hard, panic beginning to rise up in my chest. What if I was repulsive to him? What if everything Jacob had said was right and I was unattractive after all? Ryan must have sensed my fear because he took a hold of my chin and forced me to look him in the eye.

"Stop," he commanded me, his tone firm but warm, "you're overthinking things, I can see it in your eyes. You're beautiful as you are and I *want* you."

Without giving me time to think any more on what he'd just said, he pressed his lips on mine once more as he raised his hands to my breasts. Regardless of the material that covered them, he held each globe in his hands gently as his thumb teased at my nipples through the soft barrier. I arched into his hands, kissing him back hungrily now as my fears began to dissipate.

I felt my bra suddenly become slack as the clasps were undone from the back and the straps were pushed down my arms as Ryan took it off of me, the kiss remaining unbroken, giving me no chance to get scared again.

His hands reclaimed my breasts as soon as my bra was discarded somewhere onto the floor, causing me to tug impatiently at his own shirt to even the score. He complied immediately, removing his top and chucking it over his shoulder as he hurriedly replaced his hands on my breasts. I chuckled at that, feeling warm that he wanted to be touching me again so quickly.

He kneaded my breasts between his fingers, rolling them and tugging on them, the tips becoming taut under the caresses they were receiving.

Ryan moved his hands suddenly away from my breasts, curling them around my bottom instead as he lifted me up from off of the ground and carried me, taking me into his bedroom as he took one nipple into his mouth. I grabbed a hold of his head, curling my legs around his body to make it easier for him to carry me until we reached his room when he placed me gently onto his large bed, climbing onto it with me as he lavished me with his attentions.

Even through his ministrations where he appeared to be hungry for me, I couldn't believe how gentle he was being with me. This experience was fast proving to be so different to my previous encounters with my soon-to-be ex-husband and I was certain that if this was how things were with Ryan, then Jacob hadn't been as considerate of me in the past as I had thought he'd been.

I opened my eyes, watching Ryan clamber onto me as he pressed gentle kisses onto my stomach as I tried to banish all thoughts of Jacob from my mind. Ryan moved higher up my body, raising his head up to look me in the eyes. I could see the desire in them, the wanting and it made me shudder to know that someone truly wanted me like that.

My hands trailed up the sides of his torso, feeling his toned body as he kissed me once more, savouring the feel of this hot new body currently over me. I felt his hands now tugging at my trousers, trying to push them down without breaking us apart from each other.

I smiled against his mouth, lifting my hips up so

that he could push them down with more ease as I enjoyed his kisses. Within moments, I was utterly bare beneath him. It was a strange experience to encounter but it felt right. Ryan shucked his own trousers down over his hips until he sprang free of them, settling over me eagerly.

His hands were everywhere, encouraging the fire racing through me to increase as my excitement grew, my thoughts becoming jumbled as pure desire coursed through me. I heard a rustling sound and as I glanced down, I noticed the condom as Ryan placed it over himself, his arms coming back up to my shoulders as he settled over me yet again.

He lowered his head to my ear, whispering to me,

"Are you ready for me?"

"Yes," I breathed, holding myself still as I readied myself for him. He nudged gently at my entrance, allowing me to cling tightly to him as my nerves began to rear up once more and then he was surging into me, burying himself to the hilt.

I gasped as my body got used to the feel of him inside me. Ryan held himself immobile for a few seconds before he began to move. Slowly, he began to make love to me moving back and forth, his actions growing quicker with each thrust.

I clawed at his back as passion coursed through me, driving me to scream as we reached our peak together. I screamed my pleasure as I reached my climax, Ryan roaring along with me as he found his pleasure mere moments after I did.

He collapsed on top of me, panting as he pushed himself to the side and slid off of me only to then pull me into his arms tightly as he lay on the bed beside me.

I felt warm and content in his arms, safe in the knowledge that he had been thoughtful of me throughout the entire experience. My heart swelled at the knowledge and I snuggled in closer to him, feeling his warm breath upon my shoulder as his arms wrapped me in their embrace.

*   *   *

I awoke the next morning groggily.

Where was I? Things in this room were unfamiliar to what I was used to and as I thought about it, it hit me where I was. Ryan's room.

I sneaked a peek behind me, taking in Ryan's sleeping form as I glanced down at myself, realising I was fully naked beneath the sheets.

Oh God! What had I done? I could feel my cheeks heating up with embarrassment as I recalled the events of the night before. Why hadn't I stopped him? Why hadn't I been more resistant?

Even as I had the questions in my mind, I already

knew the answers. I'd *wanted* to sleep with him. I'd *wanted* him to do what he had done and it had been great. Far better an experience was had with him than I'd ever had with my husband. Guilt coursed through me as I thought of Jacob. I knew we'd broken up but a part of me felt as though I'd cheated on him. I knew it was silly to feel that way but still, the emotion was there.

Anger coursed through me then. Why should I feel guilty? I was a single woman now and what Ryan and I had shared had been wonderful. Although, he *was* Cal's brother so this might make things awkward between us all.

I rolled onto my back wide awake as I panicked over what to do. Ryan and I had crossed a line, a line that we may not be able to go back from. I brought a hand up to my face, holding my hand over my eyes as I sighed at myself. I'd made a mess of things, I just knew it.

"Everything alright?"

I jumped as Ryan spoke, his arm curling around my middle as I glanced over at him.

I gave him a weak smile.

"Yeah."

I saw a frown cross over his features at that and he raised himself up onto his right elbow so that he could gaze down at me properly.

Broken Tulips

"What is it? What's wrong?" he asked sharply.

I winced at his tone, knowing that if I told him how I felt then he'd probably be angry with me.

"Nothing's wrong," I muttered, turning my head away from him to avoid his gaze.

"Are you regretting last night? You are, aren't you?"

I sighed, turning back to him and met his gaze.

"Yes and no," I admitted, deciding the truth was the only way forwards, "it was amazing and I've never experienced making love like that before. Honestly, I haven't."

Ryan considered this for a second then spurred me on to continue.

"So what's wrong?" he questioned me.

"It sounds incredibly stupid but I feel as though I've cheated on Jacob," I allowed a moment for that to sink in, "I know that I haven't but I guess I need my heart and my head to catch up with each other you know? And then there's the fact that Cal is your brother and we will always see each other at family events over the years if things didn't work out. As much as I enjoyed myself last night with you, I can't help but think that perhaps we made the wrong move."

I registered the hurt on his face as he stared at me in disbelief, wanting the ground to swallow me up whole. I reached out to touch his arm, but then reconsidered it when I saw the way his eyes heated up instantly as my hand neared. Perhaps it was best if I didn't touch him. I pulled my hand back, sitting up and clutching the covers above my chest defensively.

"I'm sorry Ryan," I muttered apologetically, "I shouldn't have done this with you. I probably shouldn't have come here at all. I'll get dressed, get my things and go home."

I made a move to leave the bed but his hand shot out and stopped me, making me turn back to him.

"If I'm getting this right, then there's still hope for us."

I shot him a look of surprise at those words. Raising my eyebrow at him, I waited for him to continue. He took a breath first.

"Basically, what you're saying is you still need time to get over Jacob and your only other worry is if we don't work out then you'd still have to face me and you're thinking it would be awkward," he began, a philosophical expression upon his face, "I'm right aren't I?"

"Well I-," I started but he cut me off abruptly.

"So what you need is time and reassurance," he continued, "and I can provide both of those. I really like you Ellen, I've told you that before and I highly doubt my feelings are going to change *especially* after sharing such a fantastic night with you. I know you like me too but you're scared, afraid you're going to get hurt. I promise you that I won't ever hurt you intentionally...I can't promise that I won't hurt you at all because I'm a man and we tend to do things without realising it but I would never *mean* to. I can wait for you to be ready for me."

I stared at him, disbelieving this proclamation.

"You would wait for me? What if you were to find someone else whilst you were waiting for me? Wouldn't that make things awkward between us?" I pressed, knowing that he couldn't mean what he was saying.

Yet there he was, nodding his head at me emphatically.

"Yes, I would wait for you! There isn't going to be anyone else for me and I can tell you that as a fact. Do you have any idea how long I have wanted you? As soon as I knew that there were problems between you and Jacob, I hoped that you would break up so that I could ask you out! A few more months isn't going to hurt me!"

I chuckled nervously.

"You hoped we would break up?" I asked him, not too sure what to make of that. Ryan gave me a guilty smile.

"Yeah...that came out wrong. I didn't want you to be hurt but I'm glad you're free of him. You deserve someone who will make you happy and if I can be so bold, I believe that someone could be me. I'm willing to wait for you Ellen."

"But what if we didn't work out? Things would be so awkward at family events!" I squeaked, my feelings in turmoil at his admission. Was he really telling me that he would seriously wait for me? Did he truly like me that much? I barely dared to hope.

"I think we're both adult enough to at least be civil if it came to that," Ryan replied arguably, "but I honestly believe that you just need some time to think about things. It's only been a couple of weeks since your break up with Jacob and as you said, you feel guilty about sleeping with me which means you're obviously not over your relationship yet and I don't expect you to be. You were with him for a long time. As much as I'd like to be with you right now, I will wait for you until you're ready."

"And what if I'm never ready?" I countered, distracted by the sight of his naked torso as he sat up straight in the bed, leaving it to my view.

His eyes travelled to where my eyes were resting and he laughed heartily.

"I think you will be," he replied huskily, his eyes

darkening as I refocused on his face, "especially if last night is anything to go by. Shall we just say that that was something for you to look forward to when you decide you're ready?"

I blushed, feeling my cheeks heat up rapidly.

I couldn't help myself. The idea of having what we'd shared on a more frequent basis made my skin light up with desire and hope. I gave him a small smile as he watched me, his face inching closer and closer to mine.

"I'm going to have a shower! You can think of something for us to do today," I called out as I jumped from the bed and ran for the bathroom, hearing Ryan's rumble of laughter as I raced from the room. Running into the bathroom, I slammed the door shut and leaned against it breathing hard. Phew! I'd nearly kissed him then and that would have undone everything we'd just spoken about! What was it with him that drew me in so easily?

I shook my head at myself in annoyance. I needed some time to myself to move on from Jacob and to figure out who I was on my own. I owed that much to myself.

*　　　　*　　　　*

An hour later, Ryan and I were heading to the British Museum.

He explained to me that the displays changed on

occasion and the museum was a place that I simply had to visit before I went back home. He also told me that it was one of his favourite places to go to in London as it fascinated him, no matter how many times he went.

With that in mind, I felt excited to be going. When we arrived, the museum itself was enormous and the things we saw in there had me walking around in awe. It was truly magnificent and I told Ryan as much.

He grinned broadly at my enthusiasm, obviously pleased with himself.

When we finally left, several hours had passed. We had kept things light all day, not mentioning anything about the previous night or this morning but instead, pretending as though nothing had happened.

For that, I was grateful. He had understood what I wanted, respecting my wishes even as he had made it clear that he wanted me. I knew he'd said he would wait for me but I wasn't going to hold my breath. For all I knew, I was just another notch on his bedpost although I hoped that I wasn't.

For now, I was focusing on myself. We headed back to his as we couldn't decide on where to go for dinner so we figured we could decide once we were back at the flat. We played a game of pool, chatting and laughing with each other. I felt at ease around him, the like of which I had never felt with Jacob. How could there be such a difference between them? I knew I shouldn't keep comparing the two of them but I couldn't help it. The differences were huge and I couldn't believe I'd spent so many years of my life with someone who had made me feel mediocre when this one week with Ryan had made me feel like I was someone special.

The confusion inside of me kept swirling around, annoyance and hurt taking over my emotions at regular intervals. Eventually, we stopped playing pool and Ryan brought my attention back to him.

"I'm going to cook dinner," he announced, striding around to my side of the pool table.

"You are?" I asked him in surprise. So far, I had cooked or we'd had takeaways, apart from the previous evening of course. Ryan grinned at me.

"Sure! Why not? It's about time I cooked you a meal."

I gaped at him, unsure what to make of this. I wasn't used to be treated so well.

"Is there anything that I can do to help?"

Ryan shook his head, taking me by the arm and steering me towards the television.

"Nope," he replied, "I want you to sit down and relax whilst I cook you something. I'll be honest, it's only going to be meat and vegetables so I hope that's alright for you?"

"Yeah that sounds great. Thankyou," I said, watching in wonder as he made his way towards the kitchen. I'd been there less than a week and he was cooking for me. Another point for Ryan.

I shrugged my shoulders to myself as I strolled over to the tower stand that housed his dvds, perusing through the choices that were there. It seemed that Ryan preferred his comedies as there were several of those but there was also some period drama pieces in there which surprised me. I hadn't realised he liked to watch that sort of thing. I took one out and carried it into the kitchen with me, holding it up for him to see as I raised my eyebrow at his inquisitive gaze.

"Since when have you been into these types of films?" I asked curiously as a pink tinge appeared at the tips of his ears.

"Always," he replied quietly, "it's a bit of a guilty pleasure of mine."

I smiled widely at him when he said that.

"Well that's great to hear because I love watching things like this! I'm going to put it on, shall I wait for you to join me?"

Ryan visibly relaxed at my words, before telling me to go ahead and watch it as he would be cooking anyway. I left him to it and popped the disc into the player, then settled down onto the sofa to watch the period drama as it played out before me.

The film was just coming to an end when Ryan called to me that dinner was ready. I rose up from my seat, stretching once I was up and turned the film off. I headed into the kitchen and took a seat at the table that resided in there, watching Ryan as he stepped about the kitchen and prepared the food onto plates for us.

He had placed candles on the table, giving a romantic feel to the evening but that made me feel uncomfortable.

"Ryan? The candles are a nice touch and all but this isn't supposed to be a romantic dinner is it? I mean, after what we said this morning, I thought we were just going to stay friends for now."

Ryan came over to me carrying two steaming plates of food, setting one down in front of me and the other down on the opposite side of the table to me, taking his seat in the chair there.

"Don't worry, I know that's what we said. I just thought it would be a nice thing to do," he replied.

"Oh. OK," I muttered, secretly relieved that he wasn't expecting more from this.

We both tucked into our food, the delicious aroma wafting into our nostrils. He had cooked chicken with roasted vegetables and poured a smattering of gravy over the top. It was the perfect meal in my eyes. I'd always said that you couldn't beat a roast dinner. I closed my eyes briefly, savouring the taste contentedly.

"Are you enjoying your dinner?" Ryan asked me, my eyes blinking rapidly as I focused my attention on him. I noticed he had the tiniest of smiles tugging at the corners of his mouth.

"Yes it's nice thankyou," I replied primly, pretending like I hadn't just been almost drooling over it.

Ryan scoffed in amusement, not saying anything else as he returned to his food. I narrowed my eyes at him but didn't speak either. I chose to eat my food in silence, lest I made a fool of myself.

When we'd both finished, I helped him clear up. We made short work of it and made our way back in front of the television.

"It's still early enough to watch a film so would you like to choose another period drama for us to watch?" Ryan asked me, sitting down on the sofa in front of the screen and looking up at me expectantly.

I strolled over to the dvd selection, chose another film to watch and placed it in the player before going over to sit next to Ryan on the sofa.

As the film began, I found I was extremely aware of

his body next to mine, the heat radiating between us causing my hands to grow damp with sweat. Was I sweating from the heat? Or from my nerves?

We watched the film together and after a while, my nerves calmed down and I was able to watch the film with my full attention. The ending was sad, not what I had been expecting and tears were sliding down my cheeks as Ryan turned it off.

The next thing I knew, his arm was sliding around my shoulders and he was pulling me close against my side.

"Ssh, it's alright," he whispered to me, swiping at the tears with his thumb.

I sat up a little straighter, edging myself away from him as I dashed at my eyes with my hands.

"Sorry," I mumbled, "sad endings make me cry. As you can obviously see. It's silly I know."

"Not at all," he countered, "I understand how you feel. I had a few tears when I first watched that film."

I gaped at him in surprise at that admission.

"You did?"

He nodded his head slowly.

"Yep. I know it's not very manly but at least I'm not afraid to admit it. These dramas really get to me at times so that's why I have so many comedies in my selection. Sometimes I need to put one on afterwards to cheer me up."

I stared at him. I'd never known a man to admit that he cried when he saw a film like that, to openly show his sensitive side to me. Without thinking, I placed my hand upon his as my heart melted in my chest.

Ryan's face changed subtly, growing more serious but intense in the same instant as his eyes dropped to my mouth. His eyes darkened and my breath caught in my throat, my heart hammering in my chest all of a sudden.

Ryan leaned into me, his face inching closer to my own as my eyes zeroed in on his full lips, my pulse racing inside of me. My eyelids drooped as his lips touched mine softly, his hand reaching up to cup the back of my head as he pulled me in closer to him, deepening the kiss.

I gave in, kissing him back hungrily for several minutes until I realised what I was doing. Tearing myself free of him, I leapt up to my feet to put some space between us.

"We've got to stop doing this!" I cried, furious with myself at breaking my own word, "I'm not ready for this yet. I need to figure out who I am on my own and kissing you isn't going to help with that."

Ryan had the grace to hang his head in shame (or

disappointment?) at my words.

"You're right. I promised you that I would wait for you and kissing you isn't keeping that promise. You were just so irresistible that I couldn't help myself. I shall control myself until you're ready. I'm sorry."

The fight left me in a second as I gazed at his dejected form.

"Please don't think I'm not interested, you already know I am. I just need some time. OK?" I asked him hopefully.

"Of course," he replied, standing up to wrap me in his arms briefly before stepping away from me, "you know I'll wait for you Ellen."

CHAPTER ELEVEN.

I arrived back home the following day to be greeted by Cal and Lily.

Cal's face lit up when he saw me walk into the living room just as Lily chose that moment to vomit all over him. He grimaced in disgust as I tried to stifle the giggle that played upon my lips. He shook his hand before wiping it against his trousers, which were already a seemingly sorry mess upon his frame and he sighed to himself.

"Everything alright there Cal?"

I feigned my ignorance so as not to embarrass him as he threw me a dark glance.

"Things have been better, Ellen," he muttered, "Lily's been sick a couple of times this morning so I'm starting to wonder if she's caught a sickness bug or something."

I wandered closer to them and picked Lily up whilst I sat on a seat before resting her upon my knee. I gazed at the babe in my arms, noticing the sickly pallor of her face and a thin sheen of sweat upon her skin. I shifted my worried gaze over to Cal.

"Are you sure? Should we get her checked by a doctor?"

"If she doesn't get better then I'll take her but for now, I'm not going to do what most new parents do and panic. I'm sure it will pass quickly enough," Cal reassured me as he rocked back onto his heels wearily.

"Do you want to go and have a shower and clean up whilst I watch her?" I queried, offering him the chance to have a reprieve.

His grateful gaze landed on me as an exhausted smile flashed at me.

"I'd really appreciate that. I'm sorry for this poor welcome back home but I will ask you all about your trip with my brother when I'm clean and refreshed if that's alright? Thanks Ellen."

"Oh that's alright, go take care of yourself," I said to his retreating back, not sure exactly how to handle the conversation of my holiday. I was never in a million years going to tell him about Ryan and myself being intimate with each other, or the fact that I'd almost allowed it to happen again the previous evening when we'd started to kiss.

No, I would simply tell him about the places we'd been and the amazing things we had seen. He did not need to know about anything else.

I shoved the thoughts of the week to the back of

my mind as I focused all of my attention on my poorly niece. She really did look unwell, bless her little soul.

I crooned sweet lullabies to her as I rocked her gently in my arms, hoping that I was providing some comfort to her tiny form in her weakened state. Lucky for me, she did not vomit again as I held her, which I had to admit that I was grateful for but she slept instead. My lullabies had helped to send her off into a healing sleep. It was commonly known that if a person were ill, then sleep was one of the best things that could help them so I prayed that my niece would sleep for several hours in order to help heal her of her illness.

Almost an hour had passed when Cal returned down the stairs, seemingly much more refreshed than when I had seen him previously and wearing clean clothes. Indeed, he appeared to be in better spirits than he had an hour past.

When Cal saw that his daughter was asleep, he lifted her gently out of my arms and placed her into the cot that resided in one corner of the room before he faced me brightly, the relief that Lily was asleep being palpable around us.

"Ellen! How did you do it?" he queried, a smile lighting up his face as he strode over to me, lifting his arms out to me to wrap me into a warm hug. Then, he stepped back to observe me.

Broken Tulips

"I sang to her," I replied shyly, shrugging my shoulders nonchalantly.

"Ah, I see. Well, I for one am very glad that you're back. We've missed you."

My heart flipped to hear those words. It seemed silly but I was pleased to know that I had been missed, even if it was due to my ability to help out with the baby. I didn't mind that. She was family after all. Cal took a seat opposite me, gazing at me expectantly.

"So how was your trip to London? Did my brother take care of you?"

My eyes widened in alarm as he said that, making me have to calm myself down as I realised that he meant it in an innocent manner as he couldn't possibly know what had transpired between his brother and I. I cursed at myself inwardly before replying to him.

"The trip was incredible! I can't believe I've never visited the sights of London before. I'll have to go again sometime to see the things that I missed."

"I'm glad you enjoyed it! But my brother? He took care of you right?" Cal persisted, noticing that I hadn't answered that particular question.

I nodded my head hastily.

"Yes, of course he did. Perfect gentleman. He even cooked for me," I chuckled at the expression on

Cal's face at that, "I was quite honoured."

"Yes I think you were," Cal replied, laughing merrily.

We continued to catch up with each other. I told him of the places I'd been and he informed me that he had sent off my sisters' book for publication at last.

*   *   *

A month passed by in which Ryan called me a couple of times and we chatted with each other via text message but we spoke just as friends, to my relief. He didn't mention anything of what had happened between us, keeping all conversations between us light. It was kind of him not to put any pressure on me, which made me trust that he was keeping his promise to wait for me.

I continued to work hard at my job and had finally been forced to admit to my boss what was happening in my personal life as I'd had to change the address of my residence in my records. When my boss had become aware of the change, he had asked me why it had changed and so, I had been obliged to inform him of my marriage breakdown. To my surprise, he had been very understanding and had told me that if I needed any time off to deal with my emotions then he would allow it.

Broken Tulips

I thanked him, unsure what to make of his kindness. My boss was not known for being so nice but I later discovered that he had gone through a divorce of his own as his own wife had cheated on him and so he understood how I felt.

I worked even harder on my college course, hoping with all of my heart that I would pass so that I could go after the nursing degree that I wanted to do. In between work and college, I helped Cal take care of Lily and I helped take care of Cal.

He was starting to seem much better these days, looking after himself and his daughter with more ease than he had previously been doing. I decided it was time that I started to search for a place of my own to live, as I felt that Cal would be appreciate having his house back to himself.

One day, I went shopping for food so that Cal didn't need to worry about it. I strolled along the aisles as I pushed the shopping trolley, dropping things into it as I passed that I thought we might need at home.

As I turned around one end of an aisle, I came face to face with Jacob.

He stopped, staring at me as his hand dropped down from the waist of the woman he'd been holding his arm around. My eyes narrowed at them both instantly. There was the same woman who had been laying in my bed with my husband that night I had gone home and caught him out.

"Ellen! How are you?" Jacob cried, glancing nervously between the woman and myself.

"I'm alright. You?" I replied shortly, not wanting this conversation to last any longer than it needed to but I decided to be civil as I still needed him to sign the divorce papers which I knew had been served to him by now.

"Yes, very well," he answered, turning to gesture towards the woman, "this is Amelia."

The woman gave me a curt nod of acknowledgment but refused to look at me. At least I'd chosen to be civil. With Jacob, not her.

"Ah, it is lovely to meet you Amelia! I must say, you look very different with your clothes on. I take it you're sharing my marital bed with my husband on a more regular basis now?" I asked sweetly, keeping my face as pleasant as I could physically manage.

That earned me a sharp look from the both of them.

"Ellen! There's no need to be like that!"

Jacob's admonishment sounded as though he were trying to be angry but he sounded more nervous than anything. I chuckled.

"Oh, I'm not bothered Jacob! I just wish you would hurry up and sign the divorce papers so that I can be free of you. Then you can marry her if you wanted to! Now, I'll let you carry on with your day, I've got shopping to do. Bye!" I called out as I moved around them, feeling a moment of triumph at the shock I could see on their faces.

I chuckled to myself, feeling immensely proud that I had stood up to my husband and not let him win this time around. I finished my shopping with my head held high, humming a merry tune to myself as I paid the cashier and bagged up my goods. I spotted Jacob and Amelia out of the corner of my eye as I walked past the till where they were paying for their own shopping and I ignored them, strolling out past them with a smile plastered on my face.

As I put the shopping bags into the car, I heard my mobile phone ringing in my pocket. I pulled it out and answered it, registering that it was my friend Eva calling me.

"Hi! How are you?" I answered the phone to my friend with a smile. I hadn't heard from her in a long time so this was an unexpected pleasure.

"I'm good, how are you?" came the reply on the other end of the phone as I closed the car door and pushed the shopping trolley into a trolley bay.

"I'm good! To what do I owe the pleasure of this phone call?" I asked lightly, walking back to the car and getting into the driver seat. I wouldn't start up until we'd finished talking though.

"I was wondering if you fancied coming down to Devon sometime? Like a holiday? Thought you might need a change of scenery and I'd love to see you!"

I thought about it only for a moment before I replied.

"Yes, that would be great! I can book myself a long weekend off from work and come and spend a few days with you if you'd like?"

Eva agreed that we should do that and informed me that I should let her know when I could have the time off of work so that she could book the same days off too. When the phone call was ended, I hung up feeling excited.

Today was turning out to be a very good day.

CHAPTER TWELVE.

I spluttered as I laughed out loud, spitting my drink out as my friend made me laugh at the same second I took a mouthful.

The liquid went flying across the table as my friend renewed her belly laugh at my embarrassment.

"Eva! Look what you made me do!" I admonished her, even as I chuckled at the mess I'd made. She was the only person in the world who had ever made me laugh so much that I spat my drink out.

Eva shrugged her shoulders nonchalantly at me.

"What did I do? You're the one who can't handle your drink," she replied dryly, the amusement on her face belying the seriousness of her tone.

I chuckled again, shaking my head at her. We had been friends ever since I'd been at school and even though we didn't see each other very often, when we did get together it was as though we'd never been apart.

Of course I'd kept in touch with her using my mobile phone or emails but it was never quite the same as meeting up face to face. When she had offered for me to go and stay with her a few weeks before, I'd jumped at the chance. I knew that a few days with my old school friend would go a long way in making me feel better about things.

I'd arrived in Devon only that evening, about an hour before the drink spitting incident. Eva had had the wine and the food ready for us, waiting for me to arrive before getting stuck in. Considering it was only a Thursday evening, our weekend had begun.

I was lucky to have a friend like Eva. She never judged me, always offered me advice and most definitely made me laugh. She was a breath of fresh air just when I needed her. She'd managed to get the whole weekend off of work same as I had so that we could spend the entire time together catching up and having fun.

I'd arrived quite late as I'd attended my night class before leaving but Eva had waited up for me so even though it was now two in the morning, we were having a quick catch up before we went off to bed.

We didn't talk about anything deep, deciding to keep things light instead due to the fact that it was so late but Eva promised me that we were going to have a 'proper' catch up in the morning. We finished our drinks then headed off to bed, hoping to feel refreshed enough in the morning to go out for the day.

I awoke the next morning, smiling to myself as I looked about me and remembered that I was in Eva's house now. I felt as though a huge weight had been lifted from my shoulders since I'd gotten there the night before and it was an amazing feeling.

I stretched my arms above my head lazily, glancing at my phone before moving to get ready for the day. There was a message waiting for me to be read from Ryan.

'I hope you have a great weekend with your friend.'

I stared at it briefly then shaking my head, I rolled out of the bed and got ready for the day ahead.

Twenty minutes later, I sauntered down the stairs and found Eva in the kitchen at the table, eating some toast. She gestured for me to sit down as she got up and went over to the toaster, pulling some toast out and bringing it over to me.

"I heard you moving," she explained as I glanced up at her questioningly. I thanked her, taking the toast from her and beginning to eat.

We discussed what we might do that day. I let Eva choose where we should go being as this was where she lived, so she knew the best places to go. We decided to go to Powderham Castle in Exeter as Eva knew how much I enjoyed my history and castles were something I enjoyed visiting.

We left straight after breakfast, getting to the castle within an hour and began exploring. The castle itself was utterly beautiful. The castle had walls of stone but the interior held secrets that I was intrigued to discover. There was a guided tour about to start shortly after we arrived so we bought tickets and tagged along on the tour. We discovered much of the history of the castle and its' occupants during the tour as the tour guide was very passionate about their job, telling us as much as they possibly could within the tour time limit. Once it was over, I strode over to our tour guide and asked a few more questions about the history that had been thought of during the guided tour. The guide was very helpful, giving me all of the information I wanted to know before we parted ways.

After we'd walked around and taken in all of the sights, we chose to visit the Courtenay Café within the castle walls for something to eat. The inside of the cafe was pristine and beautifully decorated, the menus boasting a wide variety of wonderful foods to eat. After several minutes of indecision, Eva and I chose to go for a cream tea for two because...why not?

The cream tea arrived and my mouth salivated at the sight. We had a small pot of tea each, scones, clotted cream and jam. Mmmm, delicious! What more could we ask for? As I picked up one of the scones to start putting my cream and jam onto,

Eva cleared her throat and spoke.

"So, are you going to tell me what's been going on with you then?"

I glanced up in surprise at her, noting that she was keeping a steady eye on me now.

"I've told you the majority of it, Eva," I replied, slathering the cream onto the scone in my hands, "Jacob and I are getting a divorce, I'm living with Cal at the moment until I find somewhere else to live and I'm doing the A-level course so that I can go on to do a nursing degree when I've got the qualification I need to do so."

Eva picked up her cup of tea that she'd poured and took a sip, glimpsing me over the top of her cup. I took a bite out of my scone and moaned quietly at the fantastic taste now upon my lips.

"There's something else though isn't there?" Eva asked, setting her cup back down.

"I don't know what you mean."

I kept my gaze down, concentrating on my food. I heard a sigh of frustration erupt from Eva, catching my attention and forcing me to look back up at her.

"Ellen! I know something's bothering you! I've been your friend for far too long so I know when there's something up. So, are you going to tell me?" Eva demanded, crossing her arms across the front of her chest as she gave me a pointed glare.

I gulped. Damn, she always knew how to make me talk.

"Fine," I grumbled half-heartedly, "I slept with Ryan."

Eva's jaw went slack at that news as she openly stared at me in shock.

"You mean Cal's *brother* Ryan?" she queried, continuing to stare at me. When I nodded my head in acknowledgment, she grinned at me.

"Why are you looking at me like that?" I asked her, feeling uncomfortable at her unexpected happiness.

"That's great news! You and Ryan would be perfect for each other!"

I stared at my friend then as if she'd just grown two extra heads. Was she mad?

"How can you say that? He's my sisters' boyfriends' brother! If things didn't work out between us, can you imagine how awkward that would make things at family gatherings and the like? Plus, I'm still going through my divorce with Jacob. I shouldn't have jumped into bed with him so quickly, if at all!"

"But if he makes you happy, what does it matter?" Eva asked as she resumed drinking her tea. I sighed miserably.

"I don't want to start seeing him when I'm probably on the rebound from Jacob. It's not fair on Ryan and I need to be happy with myself first before running into another relationship. Do you know what I mean?"

I hoped she would understand. I needed her to agree with me that I'd made the right decision.

"Yes I can understand that. After all, you have to be happy with yourself as you're the one who you'll stay with your whole life...but what if Ryan is the one you are meant to be with?" Eva pointed out.

I thought about that for a couple of seconds.

"Then he will be who I end up with I guess. After we slept together, I told him I wasn't ready for anything else and he said that he would wait for me. I don't know if he will or not but so far, he's been really good about it all," I told my friend who was now munching on her own cream and jam scone. I took a sip of my tea as I waited for her answer.

"I think he will wait for you," Eva began, "when I met him at Amber's funeral, I got the feeling that he was interested in you and if he's liked you for that long, I'm pretty sure that he'll wait until you're ready. I know you like him too so it's just a matter of time. As long as you go at your pace, I can't see the problem."

"Wait, how do you know that I like him?" I asked her curiously, the confident way in which she'd said that piquing my interest.

"If you weren't into him, then this wouldn't be bothering you so much. Plus, I know you. You're interested in him," she told me firmly, her tone implying that she wasn't interested in hearing any excuses from me, "so how are things going in regards to the divorce?"

I picked up another scone then, spreading the cream and jam over it before replying to her.

"Better, I think," I told her slowly, "I saw him the other week when you invited me down here and said I wished he'd hurry up and sign the papers so that we could be free of each other. Well, I think that hit a nerve because a few days later, I got a call from my solicitor to say that Jacob had signed the papers and the wheels are finally in motion. So fingers crossed, it won't take too much longer."

"Have you agreed what each other are having out of the divorce? Are you fighting him for anything?" Eva asked me, and I shook my head immediately.

"No, I've not asked for anything," I admitted, "I didn't want things to be drawn out so I said that I just want to be free of him. We've lived most of our lives quite independently anyway so there wasn't anything to really share out. I know I probably should have demanded to have some things but I didn't want to do that. The sooner the divorce is finalised, the sooner I can move on with things. I collected the rest of my stuff already and it's in the garage at Cal's house at the moment. When I get back, I'm going to find a place for me to live."

"Well, I guess you've got to do what's right for you. It sounds like you're making a plan though so that's great! You just need to focus on yourself for now and then you can go for things with Ryan."

I laughed at the way she persisted about Ryan. She was right, I did like him and I knew that he liked me, but for now, I wanted to protect myself from any more hurt until I knew my heart could cope with it.

CHAPTER THIRTEEN.

We still had two days left together so on the Saturday morning, I asked Eva what she would like to do that day. She glanced out of the window to see what the weather was like before she gave me her answer.

"How about we go to Ladram Bay for a few hours? It's beautiful out so we might as well do some sunbathing right?" she asked me expectantly.

I cast my eye over her already tanned skin and smiled.

"As it's something you clearly love to do, then yeah why not," I agreed, gesturing at her bronzed body. Eva grinned widely at me, rubbing her hands together in glee.

"Excellent! Did you bring a bikini or anything with you?"

I shook my head, amused by the horrified expression that sprang upon her features at that news. She shook her head in what seemed like disappointment at me and came over to take me by the hand and lead me towards her bedroom.

"I've probably got something you can wear. I can't believe you didn't bring anything for the beach!"

she exclaimed, tutting at me as we strode towards her room.

"I didn't think we'd be going to the beach. How was I supposed to know?" I cried, although I was amused by her chagrin over my lack of a bathing suit.

Just half an hour later and we were setting ourselves up on the beach, laying out towels to rest upon and taking our outer clothes off so that we could get a good suntan in our bikinis. Luckily, Eva had given me a bikini that fit me reasonably well so I didn't need to feel too self-conscious about wearing it.

As I settled myself down on my towel, I gazed about me at the wonderful scene before me. The beach was sandy but with the majority of the beach made up of pebbles and stones as far as the eye could see. They weren't uncomfortable to walk on though so I didn't mind it. The sun glinted off the blue sea, the water itself lapping calmly at the shoreline as the sun beat down on everything that lay in its path. It was a truly glorious day to behold.

I raised my hand to shield my eyes from the sun as I turned my head to see further along the beach. There were several people already upon the beach, some doing the same as us and sunbathing whilst others had brought their children with them to play in the sea. There were also some large boulders standing upright in the sand at the water's edge as I looked but when I turned to ask Eva what they were doing there, I found her asleep already and snoring lightly on her towel.

I sighed in amusement and turned back to watch the waves. The only sounds I could hear were the seagulls that flew above us, the waves as they lapped against each other on the shore and the distant sounds of the other people on the beach. Other than that, it was silent. To me, it was bliss.

I closed my eyes and breathed in deeply, enjoying the peacefulness that surrounded me whilst a gentle breeze whipped through my hair. I lay back on my towel, putting my arms behind my head to cushion it and eventually, I must have dozed off as the next thing I knew, Eva was shaking me awake.

"Ellen! Come on, wake up! We gotta go!"

I grunted as I opened my eyes to look up at her.

"Why have we got to go?" I queried, rubbing my eyes before I pushed myself up into a sitting position. I noted that she'd packed our stuff up already except for the towel that I was currently sitting on.

Eva pointed upwards at the sky as she replied,

"It's gone overcast so it's probably going to rain any minute. Come on, let's go!"

I jumped up and threw my clothes on over the bikini, then grabbed my towel and bag up from off of the floor and we ran over to the car, making it inside the vehicle just as the first fat drops of rain landed on the windows.

"Phew!" Eva chuckled, "we made it just in time. I was thinking, being as sunbathing is off the menu now, why don't I take you to Exeter Cathedral?"

"Yeah, sure," I agreed, thinking to myself that it would be lovely to see the cathedral even though it was a shame that our beach session had come to an end early. I took a look at the time and noticed it was midday. We'd been on the beach all morning! I hadn't realised I'd slept for so long.

It took us a little over forty minutes to get from Ladram Bay to Exeter Cathedral as the traffic was busy due to it being the weekend. Eva assured me that usually it only took half an hour to get there but not this day.

As we pulled up into the carpark, I stared up at it in awe. The cathedral was enormous yet beautiful to witness. We walked slowly inside, remaining silent in reverence of the place of worship and I couldn't help but ogle the resplendent interior as we made our way around.

People were sat praying as we passed by, ignorant to the world around them as they showed their faith. Eva and I moved slowly around the cathedral, taking in the rich history that it showed and staring in wonder at the stained glass windows and the sculpted figures that lay hidden around various bends.

There was a small shop in the cathedral so I wandered over and perused the items that they sold, eventually picking up one of the books that told of the history of the cathedral. It seemed as though it would be an interesting read so I paid for it, putting it into my bag as we left.

"Wow Eva, I can't believe you have so many beautiful places on your doorstep! And the history is so rich! I love it," I enthused to my friend as we clambered back into her car.

Eva just laughed at me as she started the engine and drove off, heading in the direction of home.

"I knew you'd love the cathedral," she told me as she drove along.

"Well, you do know me pretty well," I replied, a smile lingering upon my lips.

When we reached her house, we went back inside and got ready for a night out. Eva had already told me that she'd planned to take me to the local pub for a few drinks so once we were ready, we headed to the pub. It was only a ten minute trek to the nearest pub so we went by foot, knowing that our stumble home would be cheaper by not having to order a taxi.

We strolled into the pub to be greeted by some ruddy faced locals whom were already laughing merrily with each other. Several of them turned towards us as we went inside and a few men in the corner waved us over.

"Eva! Come over here with us!" they called out.

I raised my eyebrow at my friend but she clicked her tongue and tugged my arm as she pulled us over to the men that were calling to her.

"Hi gents! Who's buying us the first round then?" she asked with a large smile plastered upon her face.

"Me!" claimed one of the men as he stood up and asked us what we'd like to drink. We sat ourselves down at their table whilst the man went to fetch our drinks and Eva introduced me to the man that remained seated at the table.

"Ellen, this is Jack. The fella that went to get our drinks is Toby," she announced, smiling warmly at Jack. If I didn't know her better, I would say that my friend had a bit of a crush on the man sat in front of us.

Our drinks appeared a few minutes later, courtesy of Toby. I thanked him and took a sip of my wine as Eva launched into conversation with Jack and Toby. I sat and listened, contributing to the conversation only when necessary until Toby turned towards me, leaving Eva and Jack to carry on with what they were saying.

"So, you're here for a visit?" Toby asked me, leaning in towards me. I nodded my head.

"Yeah, I needed to get away for a few days and Eva offered me a place to stay," I answered, sipping on my wine that he'd bought for me.

As they had all been talking, I'd rapidly discovered that they were all firm friends and that Eva sat with them often when she was in the pub. Apparently, there were some others from the area that came and joined them for a drink if they were about but it didn't seem like they were this time. It was great to see that my friend had a good bunch of people whom she could spend time with in Devon. I'd always worried that being on her own she might be lonely, but this weekend alone had proven to me that she was more than happy as she was and that she had friends whom she could spend time with. I didn't need to worry about her.

"Oh dear, that sounds ominous," Toby said, smiling at me, "why did you need to get away? If you don't mind me asking of course."

I took a deep breath, deciding honesty was the best policy here.

"I'm going through a divorce. We've been separated for a little while now and we should've ended things a long time ago but we tried to make it work," I replied, keeping my eyes trained on the

Broken Tulips

glass in my hands so that I couldn't see his face. I hated the expression of pity people gave me whenever I told them about my divorce. I knew they meant well but it was just a constant reminder that my marriage had failed.

"Ah, I see. At least you tried," Toby said, keeping his tone light which made me glance up at him in surprise. There was no pity in his eyes. I studied him as he picked up his beer and took a long swig of it before he returned to our conversation.

"So you realised that he wasn't the one for you? What happened to make you realise it?" he asked me.

"I went home one night and found him with another woman in our bed. Needless to say, there was no going back from that," I replied bluntly, unsure of where this conversation was heading.

I took a peek over at Eva but she was lost in talking with Jack. A nervous tremor shivered through me then as Toby shifted slightly closer to me in his seat, causing our knees to brush against each other. I sincerely hoped this wasn't going to go the way I had a feeling it would. He was a nice guy seemingly but I wasn't interested in him. And I didn't know him.

"So have you been with anyone since you and your husband split up?" Toby muttered quietly, leaning his head closer to my ear.

"I'm not sure that's any of your business," I replied, pulling myself away from him as the uneasiness inside of me grew.

"That means you have then," he said, a wicked grin spreading across his face, "would you consider spending some time with me perhaps?"

"No. I wouldn't," I told him firmly, standing up to put some space between us and turned to Eva, "I think we should move on to the next pub Eva, what about you?"

Eva started with surprise and looked up at me, then she turned her gaze onto Toby and narrowed her eyes.

"Are you being a pig again Toby? What have you done?" she demanded.

Toby held his hands up in feigned innocence, stating that he hadn't done anything so Eva asked me what had happened. When I told her, she whirled back on to Toby, her anger with him palpable in the air.

"You idiot! She tells you that she's going through a divorce and you come on to her like some stupid horn dog?! Come on Ellen, let's get out of here," she ordered, standing up and grabbing her bag. Just before we left, she stood right up to Toby and spat,

"I'll be having words with you next time I see you!"

And with that, we left.

I felt guilty as I hadn't wanted to cause a scene but Toby had made me feel uncomfortable and I'd forgotten how protective of me Eva could be.

I smiled as I walked alongside her, grateful that she was there to help me. Why did men always have to try and 'have' you when they discovered you were single? Especially when you're in the middle of a divorce? I didn't want it and the very thought of it with that Toby had made me shudder.

I realised that Eva had been right about one thing though. I really did like Ryan. The incident that night had proven it to myself. Now I just had to concentrate on taking care of myself before I went down that road with him. Again.

CHAPTER FOURTEEN.

Eva and I spent the Sunday of that weekend at hers, in the garden, lapping up the sunshine whilst it lasted and drinking wine.

In the morning, we had both been nursing hangovers from the amount of alcohol that we'd drunk on the Saturday night when we'd moved onto the next pub but one greasy full English breakfast later with some orange juice and we were ready for what the day had to throw at us.

As the sun was out, we'd poured ourselves some wine and gone into the garden, lounging on Eva's garden chairs and placing the bottle of wine we were drinking from on the small table that was next to Eva's chair.

I glanced over at Eva and smiled, letting her take a sip of her drink before I spoke.

"So," I began as she leant back in her seat, "what's the deal with you and Jack?"

Eva's cheeks flushed pink even as she tried to pretend like she didn't know what I was talking about.

"What do you mean?"

I chuckled at her. Had she not been preaching to

me about Ryan a mere twenty four hours ago? And now she was feigning ignorance when I brought up Jack?

"You are totally into him! Don't even try to deny it lady!" I exclaimed, putting my hands up to stop her protests before she could start, "so when were you going to tell me about him?"

Eva had the good grace to look slightly guilty at that but shrugged it off quickly.

"I wasn't. We're just friends," she replied defensively, squaring her shoulders and taking another sip of her wine.

"Oh Eva! I can see you're just friends but I can also see that you like him. Has he got a partner already?" I asked, determined to get to the bottom of this.

"No he hasn't."

"So why are you holding back? I've never known you to hold back from something that you've wanted before."

Eva waved her hand at me as though she were trying to wave me away before she replied,

"I don't know if it's a good move for us. Yeah I like him and he likes me, but we may be better off as friends."

"Is that what you really think?" I asked her in stupefication. I couldn't remember the last time Eva had been unsure about something, she was usually so confident and outgoing.

"Yeah. Plus, there's his friend Toby," she glanced to me at that, "I'm sorry about him by the way. He tried it on with me when I first met him and I forgot to warn you about that."

I smiled at her in reassurance.

"It's alright don't worry. I probably reacted worse than normal too being as I'm a bit sensitive to everything at the moment, although I've got to be honest, Toby isn't exactly the best looking guy so what made him think that that was acceptable?"

Eva shook her head in the manner of someone who doesn't know the answer.

"I don't know. He's always been like it. He probably assumed that you would be desperate for some attention considering the whole divorce thing, but then, he doesn't know about Ryan either," Eva told me, a wicked grin replacing the frown upon her face.

"Nuh uh!" I pointed my finger at her, "we are not going back there right now. We are talking about you and Jack, not Ryan. Why don't you go out on a date with him and just see how it goes?"

Pleased to see that I'd managed to evade the subject of Ryan, I waited for her answer. Eva's shoulders slumped and she pouted, apparently thinking about the scenario.

"OK I guess we could try that," she acquiesced, "but what if it goes horribly wrong? Then my whole group of friends here would become very limited and awkward."

I thought about this. Then I turned to her.

"Do you think it will go horribly wrong?" I asked.

"No," she admitted after a few seconds, "I think it would probably go pretty well but what if it doesn't?"

"Then it doesn't," I told her bluntly, "but are you willing to deny yourself this chance at love simply because you're not willing to try?"

Even as I said the words, I could feel the irony as it reflected my own situation with Ryan. I *was* willing to try, just not yet.

*   *   *

I'd been home from Devon for a week when I was able to get a viewing on a house in the same village as Cal's. He'd already told me that I could stay at his for as long as I wanted but I explained to him how I needed my own space. I was sure he understood but I had the feeling he wanted me to stay. Perhaps to take care of the house? Who knew?

I went and saw the house to see if it was something I'd be interested in. Unfortunately, it was a place to rent but I didn't have a choice, I didn't earn enough to be able to get a mortgage by myself.

It had a decent sized living room, a large kitchen, two bedrooms and a bathroom. It was all I needed and it was within my price range. I said yes to renting it.

When I arrived back at Cal's, I told him the good news. Cal smiled at me, pulling me into a bear hug and asked me when I would be moving into my new place. I had to wait for the owner of the building to get back to me so I informed him that I wasn't sure but I would let him know as soon as I did know.

*   *   *

Moving day.

I was finally moving into my new place, my new home and I was feeling very excited. Thankfully, most of my things were already boxed up and hiding in Cal's garage as that was where I'd stored them when I collected my things from the house I'd shared with Jacob so at least there wasn't much for me to pack. However, I would have to unpack everything once I was inside the house so I wasn't looking forward to that so much.

Cal had offered to help me but I'd politely refused as he needed to look after my niece and he couldn't very well do that if he was helping me to move house so he called for some help. Yep, you guessed it. He called Ryan to come and help me to move house so that I didn't have to do it by myself and struggle.

So as I packed up my remaining clothes and bathroom bits that I'd left unpacked for my last night at Cal's, I heard a car pull up on the driveway and minutes later, Ryan was being greeted at the front door by Cal.

Much to my annoyance, I could feel my pulse racing and my heart beating faster at the thought of seeing Ryan. I rolled my eyes at myself, silently scolding myself for having such a reaction to him.

"Concentrate on yourself," I muttered under my breath to myself as I picked up my bag that I'd just packed and made my way down the stairs.

I found Ryan in the living room, leaning against the kitchen doorway with his arms folded across his chest as he waited for me. His whole face seemed to light up as soon as he saw me, the lazy smile upon his face widening instantly.

"Ellen! Good to see you," he said in welcome, even as he strode over to me and gave me a quick hug.

"It's good to see you too, Ryan," I replied, giving him a small smile but avoiding his gaze where I could.

I noticed that he faltered, unsure of what to make of me when I didn't look at him but he quickly recovered. He plucked my bag from out of my hands and said,

"I'm here to do the lifting. Shall we get started?"

I nodded my head, turning to walk outside towards the garage with Ryan following me. I chucked my car keys to him, announcing that he could put the bag in my car before coming to collect some more of my things from out of the garage. He did so without saying anything.

I felt a little bit guilty that I was probably coming across as a bit of a cow but I was feeling nervous around him again, trying to act normal but failing miserably.

"Just concentrate on moving," I muttered as I opened the garage door to gain access to my boxed stuff. I stared at the boxes miserably, there were only six boxes in there of mine.

I sighed to myself, not noticing when Ryan came to stand just behind me until his hand was rested upon my shoulder. I jumped in surprise but seeing who it was, I relaxed.

"Jeez Ryan! You scared me!"

He chuckled, pressing closer to me so that I could feel the deep rumble vibrating from his chest. I leaned backwards into him, sighing as I caved for just a moment.

"I didn't mean to scare you," he whispered into my ear, his warm breath blowing against me, causing my body to tremble until I realised what I was doing and stepped forwards away from him. I cleared my throat as I bent to pick up one of the boxes.

"We need to get cracking, come on," I told him, hurrying away from him and praying that he wouldn't see the blush that I was certain was beginning to creep across my cheeks. I heard another low chuckle from him as he bent to pick up a box and followed me to my car. Another couple of trips from the garage to the car and everything was inside the vehicle, awaiting its' new home.

Ryan hopped into the passenger side as I climbed into the drivers' seat and we headed off to my new house. It only took a couple of minutes to get there being as it was only a few streets away from Cal but the car had made it easier to transport everything.

We made quick work of taking the boxes inside, leaving them in the living room and I went to get us both a can of soda from out of the fridge which I'd already stocked up with food and bits I would need.

I handed Ryan his drink as he studied his surroundings, turning to me with a raised eyebrow.

"Where's all your things?" he asked.

"What do you mean? Everything of mine is here," I reminded him by gesturing towards the boxes that we'd just carried inside.

Ryan frowned at me then.

"No, I mean, where's your sofa? Your table? You know, all of that kind of thing?"

"Oh! I see what you mean! Most of that stuff is arriving tomorrow, including the bed but I still need to go and buy an airbed for tonight and cushions and bedsheets and the like. I'll be doing that today at some point," I replied, amused by the expression on his face. He looked positively horrified.

"What? How come you haven't got any of those things?" he asked, his brow furrowed as he wondered why my furniture was so minimalistic.

"I've never had to buy them. Everything I used before is currently in Jacob's house and I didn't need to buy anything at Cal's so that's why it's all new here. I've had to restart from scratch."

I could see the second when the realisation dawned upon him. He'd not thought about the fact that my husband still had everything that was needed for a house. He'd assumed I'd have some furniture already.

"I'm so sorry Ellen, I didn't think," he apologised.

"Don't worry. Maybe you can come with me to help pick things out? Unless you've got to get back home of course?" I asked him, wondering why I was inviting him to help me shop for my new abode even as I spoke the words.

The heat in his gaze as he answered yes made me regret the decision even more. What was I doing? I mentally scolded myself for playing with fire, even as I realised that I was secretly glad that he was accompanying me. Ugh! Why couldn't I think straight when he was around?

I stalked out to the car with Ryan following me. An awkward twenty minutes later and we were at the local supermarket store.

"Are you getting what you need from here?" Ryan asked me, unable to hide the astonishment on his face.

"Yeah why?" I asked him, laughing at the baffled expression he gave me.

"Can you get everything you need from here? I thought you'd need to go to lots of shops."

I laughed at him again as I shook my head.

"No, no. I'll get the majority of things that I need from here and then perhaps go to another store if there's anything missing," I informed him, taking a trolley from the trolley bay nearest to us and pushed it inside the store with Ryan by my side.

We ambled around slowly as I chose bedsheets, lamps, cushions for my new sofa and a kettle. We picked up some cutlery along the way and a tableware set with matching cups.

Luckily, I found everything that I needed to find in just the one shop so after I paid for everything, we carted it all back to my car. After it was all in, we set off for my home.

"I still can't believe you've managed to get everything you needed from just one shop," Ryan told me, shaking his head whilst still trying to comprehend it.

I chuckled.

"Why?" I asked him, amused by his reaction.

"Well, no offense intended, but most women take forever to choose what they want and usually go to lots of different shops to get the best deal."

"Ah, I see," I began, "so you're surprised that I'm more efficient than the women you've known before and managed to do my shopping in a short amount of time?"

"In a nutshell, yeah," Ryan answered, unable to hide the grin that was teasing his lips at that.

We continued on in companionable silence until we reached my new home. We took the bags out of the car and carried them inside, dumping them on the ground in the living room with the rest of my things.

"Thanks for helping me Ryan," I told him, turning to face him.

"You're welcome. What do you want me to do next?" he asked me as he came to stand closer to me.

I shook my head before replying to him.

"Nothing. You can go home now if you'd like to, unless you're staying at Cal's. Thankyou for all of your help."

Silence descended upon us as Ryan stared at me. He looked as though I'd punched him in the gut, although I couldn't think how I might have offended him.

"That's it?" he spluttered after a couple of minutes.

"Yes....you've helped me move my stuff in and there's nothing more to be done now until my delivery of furniture arrives. What were you thinking was left to do?"

Ryan took another step closer to me, his arm gesturing towards the bags and boxes of things that were filling my living room.

"Don't you want to have all of this put away? Or at least stored somewhere else until the furniture arrives?"

I gazed about me at the things he was pointing at, feeling rather stupid that I hadn't thought about him helping me with them.

"Oh, well I didn't think you'd want to do that. I mean, it would definitely be easier if you helped me but I wasn't expecting you to help me unpack," I told him, stumbling over my words as I realised why he'd been so hurt by my dismissal of him. He'd blatantly thought I just wanted rid of him. Oops, my mistake.

"Of course I'd like to help you unpack," Ryan told me, taking my hand in his, "it's what I'm here for. To do your bidding."

He said this last with a smile upon his face as he lifted my hand to his mouth and pressed a gentle kiss against my knuckles.

I cleared my throat and thanked him. I pulled my hand away and turned to have a look in the boxes that we'd brought into the house first. I asked if he would mind taking them all upstairs with me, as most of the things were either my clothes which would be in my bedroom or personal items that were more sentimental than anything else so they would go into the attic for the time being.

Ryan obliged, promptly carrying a box upstairs whilst I followed behind him. I pointed out the room which was to be my bedroom and we headed in there, placing our boxes onto the floor.

"You stay here and figure out where you want which boxes and I'll fetch the rest," he told me, already disappearing back down the stairs before I had a chance to answer him.

I stood for a moment, taking the chance to close my eyes and breathe deeply to calm myself. Being in such close proximity to Ryan for this long was causing me to have flashbacks to our night together, continuing to fan my uneasiness around him as I tried my best not to do anything I would regret. Again. Not that I regretted our night together but I did wish it hadn't happened as I wouldn't suddenly be feeling as hot as I did whenever I was near him.

"You alright?"

I started at the voice, realising I'd been daydreaming for longer than I'd realised and Ryan had made it back upstairs with another box. He was gazing at me now in concern as he placed the box on the floor and strode over to me.

"Yeah I'm fine," I replied briskly, trying to shake the naked image of him that I had in my mind away.

Ryan reached my side and lifted his hand to my face, cupping my cheek in his palm as he stroked his thumb across my chin.

"What's wrong?" he murmured, forcing me to look him in the eye as he raised my chin up.

My heart skipped a beat as his eyes bore into mine.

"Nothing's wrong," I mumbled, my tongue darting out to lick my lips without realising it until his eyes shifted and zeroed in on my mouth. Uh oh. I'd seen that gaze before.

I gulped as I placed my hands onto his chest and pushed. Not hard enough that he would go flying backwards but hard enough to know that we weren't going to go there this time.

Ryan's brow furrowed but he didn't say anything. He turned and went off down the stairs, returning within minutes with another box.

"We should probably get this lot sorted," he said brightly as I studied him to see if he was angry with me. I didn't think he was so I figured I'd see how things went as time went on.

Ryan put the boxes up into the attic which I asked him to and then I reassured him that I could do the rest by myself as they were just clothes. Once we were done, I drove him back to Cal's house so that he could either stay at Cal's or go home. I wasn't sure what he had planned but the least I could do was drive him back.

"Can you get out of the car for a few minutes Ellen? I've got something for you," Ryan asked me as we parked up.

"You have?" I asked in surprise, getting out of the

car whilst Ryan got out and went over to his own car. Reaching inside, he pulled a small box from the backseat of his car and turned to face me. It was wrapped in pretty purple paper with a neat little bow tied around it.

Curious, I strolled over to him and took the gift that he offered to me. Glancing back up at him, I quirked my eyebrow.

"You got me a gift?" I asked.

"Yeah, I did," he replied, a small smile finally returning to his face, "and after seeing your new home today, I'm pleased to see that you haven't got one."

I chortled at that, wondering what it was that he'd bought for me. I opened the paper and the box that it hid in seconds, opening it up to discover a vintage style figurine clock. It was bronze in colour with painted flowers all around its frame. I gazed back up at Ryan in wonder.

"Thankyou, it's beautiful!"

Ryan grinned at me.

"I had a feeling you might like it."

He leaned in close to me then and with his face only inches from mine, he descended upon me. His lips pressed against mine softly as his arms wrapped around me, holding me close until he broke away from me.

"I'm sorry, but I couldn't hold that in anymore," he muttered, the tips of his ears turning pink as he rubbed one of his hands against the back of his neck, "I wanted to kiss you so much back at your house but you pulled away. I know you're not ready and feel free to slap me if I was out of order but that kiss was worth whatever happens next."

I stared at him, moved by his words. He'd risked it even though he'd thought I might slap him? I smiled shyly.

"I'm not going to slap you, Ryan. Thanks for your help and for the gift, it's lovely. See you around."

And with that, I walked away with a smile upon my face that did not want to fade.

CHAPTER FIFTEEN.

A few weeks later and I was back at Cal's house, ready for a week-long stay to babysit my niece whilst Cal went on a book signing tour to promote Amber's last book.

It had finally been published and he needed to advertise it whilst meeting his fans. It had been a long time since he'd done a book tour and spoken with his fans face to face so it was time he did so, which meant I needed to come and babysit his daughter.

Due to the fact that I couldn't get the time off from work to be there during the day, Ryan had also agreed to come and stay at Cal's house so that we could share the responsibility between us and he would babysit during the day. It also allowed me to continue with my night classes being as Ryan would be around.

Ryan had already arrived by the time I'd gotten to Cal's and my heart sped up at the sight of him. I'd been thinking a lot about him and our mutual feelings, wondering whether I should indeed give things a try between us and take the chance on us.

I'd received some news that had made me think even more about it and even though I didn't want to be trapped in another relationship when I'd only just come out of one, I also realised that Ryan wouldn't be like that. From everything I knew about him, I knew that he would help me to flourish and grow in my life instead of holding me back with insecurities. So after a lot of soul searching, I had finally come to a decision about Ryan. About us. I just needed the guts to go ahead with it.

Cal had greeted me with a big smile, wrapping me in his arms for a hug before taking me over to Lily who was playing on a musical mat on the floor. He picked his daughter up and gave her a long cuddle and a kiss on the forehead before he said his goodbyes to us.

I walked him to the door so that I could tell him my news before he left on his tour and tugged on his arm to make him turn back to me.

"I know you'll be back in a week but I wanted to let you know now, I've got my divorce through at last. It's been finalised and I'm officially a single woman now," I informed him, struggling to hide the smile that wanted to break free. Cal's happy smile that was returned to me made me breathe a sigh of relief.

"That's great news! I'm so pleased to hear it!" he exclaimed, giving me yet another hug, "does this mean you'll go for it with my brother now?"

I stared at him, openmouthed, unsure what to say.

Had Ryan told him about us?! I knew I certainly hadn't. Cal chuckled at the sight of my face, continuing on,

"I'm sorry Ellen but any idiot can see that you two fancy the pants off of each other! I can promise you, he would treat you right. Nothing like your dickhead ex did."

"Um, I didn't realise it was so obvious?" I stated, still utterly gobsmacked by what he'd said, "so you wouldn't mind?"

Cal looked incredulous at that question.

"Mind? Why on earth would I mind? You both deserve someone to make you happy and I can't think of anyone better suited for each other. Just promise me one thing, don't go scarring my daughter by making out in front of her alright?" he told me, winking as he did so, so that I knew he was joking. Kind of.

"Right, I'll be back next Saturday so enjoy the weekend and your week without me and I'll see you next week! Bye!" he called out, already making his way up the path to go to the car waiting for him to take him on his book tour.

I chuckled as I shook my head at him, suddenly feeling as though a weight had lifted off of my chest. I realised that I'd been scared of what Cal might say about Ryan and myself if we did go out with each other but now I knew that Cal had no problem with it, that he'd actually made it clear that he would be happy about it, I had nothing stopping me from just going for it. Yes, there were many things that could go wrong but then again, there were many things that could go right. We'd just have to roll with it.

I went back inside to where Ryan and Lily were both playing on the floor and I joined them, unable to stop smiling. Ryan noticed and quirked his eyebrow at me.

"Everything alright? You seem pretty happy," he observed as he handed a small maraca to our niece.

"Yeah, I'm good. I just had a quick chat with Cal and he made me feel better," I replied, glancing up at him as he turned his face to me.

"Feel better about what? Was something wrong?" he asked, concern lacing his tone.

"No, nothing's wrong don't worry. In fact, things are looking up!"

I could tell he was uncertain what I was talking about but I knew I could explain things to him later on. For now, I wanted to play with my gorgeous niece. She truly was a beautiful baby, although I couldn't really call her a baby anymore as she had grown so much. She was crawling now and even beginning to say some of her first words. I knew that her mother would have been so proud of her and it saddened me to know that Amber wasn't here with us.

* * *

That afternoon, Ryan and I had taken Lily to the park, playing with her and enjoying hearing her laughter as she giggled as she played. We couldn't do too much as she wasn't old enough yet to play on everything but she seemed to really like the baby swings that were there.

Ryan had pushed her whilst I'd spent the whole time worrying that she might fall out. Silly I knew but I couldn't help it.

Hours later and Lily was in bed, her baby monitor on so that we could hear her if she woke up and Ryan and I had just ordered a takeaway for ourselves because neither of us could be bothered to cook.

I sat on the sofa as Ryan fetched us both a couple of drinks. When he returned, I decided it was time to tell him about my divorce and about how I felt.

"Thanks," I murmured as he handed me my drink and sat down next to me on the sofa.

My nerves were running rife inside of me, causing my hands to shake a little, something which didn't go unnoticed by the hunky man sat beside me.

"Are you alright Ellen? Your hands are shaking," he

asked me, reaching over and touching my arm in a concerned manner.

"Yes, I'm fine," I assured him, taking a quick sip of my drink before facing him, "although I do have something to tell you."

"Uh oh, that sounds ominous," he quipped, attempting to make me smile. It worked, but only slightly.

"I thought I should let you know that my divorce is finalised now. I'm officially no longer married to Jacob."

His whole face lit up immediately, quickly replaced by concern. And was that worry I could see?

"That's great news," he said, "you must be happy to finally be free of him."

I nodded my head, glancing down at the drink in my hands as I took a deep breath.

"Yes I am," I replied, not looking up, "and I've also been thinking about us."

He stilled, unmoving as I dragged my eyes back up to look at him. I couldn't read his face but I could see that he was waiting for me to continue.

"I know I asked you to wait and you've done exactly that. I'm sorry that I have taken so long to sort my head out but I needed the time to make sure that one, I wasn't rushing into anything and two, I was doing the right thing. What I'd like to know from you before I say anything else is this- do you still want to be with me?" I asked him, keeping my eyes trained on his face even as I had every urge to look away. Now was not the time to be a coward.

"Yes, you know I do," he muttered, his back straightening a little in the seat he was in.

"Well I'm pleased to hear that because I've thought about it, and I'm willing to try. I can't keep saying no to you. There's obviously something between us and I'd be an idiot not to take a chance on us."

There was a moment of silence then as Ryan took in what I'd just said. A couple of seconds passed. Ryan glanced back at me then, a smile stealing over his features.

"You're willing to take a chance on us?" he asked quietly, apparently double-checking that I'd said that.

At my nod of the head, the smile took over his face completely. I held my hand up quickly.

"But we can't do anything here whilst we're looking after Lily. I don't want it to interfere with our babysitting ok?"

I hoped he would understand me. To my delight, he did.

"I can agree to that. As long as you agree to go on a date with me next Saturday night when Cal is back and we aren't babysitting anymore?" Ryan asked me, taking my hand in his lightly.

"OK. Sounds like a good idea to me," I acquiesced, loving the feel of his hand on mine.

Ryan shifted his body so that he was fully facing me where we sat.

"I'd also like to kiss you now, if you'll let me," he muttered, taking his other hand and cupping my face in his palm. I leaned into his hand as I murmured my agreement and waited, my eyes locked on his mouth as it moved towards mine.

Those luscious full lips were something I had been craving, ever since that last kiss we had shared a few weeks past. His tongue darted out to lick his top lip as he came closer to me, moistening them ready for me. I placed my hand on his chest feeling the strong muscle underneath before I caught a hold of the front of his shirt and pulled him closer, causing his lips to meet mine on a faster descent than he had planned.

Our lips crashed together, the kiss instantly electrifying my body as emotions of desire and passion coursed through me. Ryan kissed me back ardently, unable to hide his own passion as the kiss grew harder, more feverish. His tongue pushed at the seam of my mouth and I opened my lips, allowing him access to me as I thrust my own tongue into his mouth.

We shared this deep kiss for several minutes before we finally broke apart, panting slightly from the heat of it.

I could see that Ryan's eyes were glowing as he grinned at me. This could turn out to be a very interesting week.

CHAPTER SIXTEEN.

That week turned out to be a great week.

After our kiss, Ryan and I had sat and watched a film whilst eating our takeaway once it had arrived. The next day, we took Lily to the zoo. There was a zoo about forty five minutes from where Cal lived so we took her there. Lily appeared to enjoy seeing the animals but I had to admit, it was probably an activity that we should have done with her when she was older. Ryan and I had enjoyed it however, and we'd taken lots of photographs to show Lily when she was old enough.

When we had gone home, we had cooked dinner and spent a nice evening together with Lily sleeping downstairs with us until we went up to bed ourselves because she had been unsettled.

I was sleeping in the spare room while Ryan slept in Cal's bedroom. Ryan had asked if I wanted to change rooms so that I could have the larger bed but I'd declined, saying I was content in the spare room.

The week itself passed by quite quickly. I was at work all day and Ryan would usually have emails and phone calls to catch up on during the evenings in regards to his own job so we didn't see very much of each other through the week. I decided that was probably the best thing to have happened because then we couldn't be distracted by each other.

As the week progressed and on the evenings when I was there (apart from the nights I had college classes), I sat down and read the book that my sister had last written which Cal had finished for her.

I'd wanted to know what she had written for so long that I'd spent the first half an hour simply gazing at the book, almost afraid to open it. I'd taken a breath and opened the book, beginning to read.

It took me all week to finish reading it, what with having to work, study and babysit but finally on the Friday evening, I read the last page just as Ryan walked into the living room.

"Hey, what's the matter?" he asked, rushing over to me and taking a seat next to me.

Tears were trailing their way down my face as I had been unable to hold them at bay. For a minute, I couldn't speak. I could only cry so Ryan pulled me into his arms, resting his chin upon the top of my head as he held me tightly, waiting for the tears to subside. It took a few minutes for me to calm down some, but when I did I pulled back and wiped at the tears on my face with the back of my hand.

"Sorry," I mumbled, "I didn't mean to get your

shirt wet."

Ryan shook his head, gazing at me in wonderment.

"I'm not bothered about the shirt, Ellen. What's happened?" he asked, taking one of my hands in his.

"It's nothing really," I sniffled, beginning to feel a bit foolish, "I've just finished reading Amber's book. Have you read it?"

Understanding flooded across his face as he glanced down to see the book that still lay upon my lap. He sighed as he pulled me against his body, wrapping his arms around me as he held me close.

"Yeah I've read it," he murmured into my hair as my tears slowly subsided. I sniffled against his shoulder until I was able to calm myself fully, then I pulled back once more.

"I'm sorry," I mumbled.

"It's alright. She was your sister and those are her last words so I completely understand. Why don't you go up and have a bath to relax yourself and I'll stay down here to keep an ear out for Lily on the monitor? I'll cook us some dinner as well. I know we haven't seen much of each other this week due to one thing or another so being as it's our last night here, why don't we make a celebration of it?" Ryan asked me brightly, trying his best to cheer me up.

Broken Tulips

I gave him a small smile as I agreed, getting up and going up the stairs into the little bathroom. Perhaps a nice hot bath would soothe me.

I ran the bath, giving myself lots of bubbles so that I would be covered when I got into the tub. I'd always liked lots of bubbles in my baths when I had them so I knew I would enjoy this one. Once it was ready, I undressed and sank into the hot bath, sighing in contentment as I closed my eyes and laid back in the tub. I didn't know how long I laid there but by the time I got out of the tub, my skin had wrinkled from the water.

I chuckled at that as I dried myself off then wrapped the towel around myself to walk into the room I'd been staying in, only to come to an abrupt stop as soon as I'd stepped out of the bathroom. There, in front of me, was Ryan. He must have just come out of the room that Lily was in but the second that he saw me, he froze, his hand still on the doorknob of Lily's room.

"Er, hi," I greeted, clutching my towel even tighter against my body as I was very aware of the fact that the towel was the only thing protecting me from his view.

"Hi," Ryan returned, "I was just checking on Lily. I heard her gurgling on the baby monitor so thought I ought to...how was your bath?"

"Yeah, it was just what I needed. Thanks," I replied,

wondering if he was ever going to move or if I was going to have to walk past him like this to get to my room.

I saw him gulp as his eyes travelled up and down the length of my body, taking me in even as I dripped water onto the carpet below my feet. He stepped closer to me then, shortening the distance between us in just a couple of strides.

"You're beautiful," he whispered, his face just inches from my own. My breath hitched as he lowered his mouth to mine, capturing it with his own as he pressed a kiss against my lips gently at first, growing more urgent with each second that passed.

His fingers trailed across my bare shoulders causing a shiver to travel down my spine as I moaned into his mouth, enjoying the kiss as it swallowed me whole. I felt a rumble in his chest as he groaned slightly, deepening the kiss with fervour.

A cry sounded, loud and long as we yanked ourselves apart from each other, listening intently as we waited to see if we heard the sound again. A second later, the cry came again. I groaned inwardly as I realised it was Lily. What was I thinking? I shouldn't be kissing Ryan when Lily was in bed a mere few feet away. I sighed as I glanced back at Ryan who gave me a sheepish grin.

"I'll go back and check in on Lily. You get dressed

and I'll meet you downstairs," he told me boldly, before disappearing into the room he had not long come out of.

I breathed a small sigh of relief as I made my way into the bedroom I was staying in and closed the door behind me. Phew! That had been a close call. The sparks between us flew almost every time that we were together and I had no doubt in my mind that the following night would probably end up with us in bed together, especially if what had just happened was anything to go by. As much as I had tried to avoid it for as long as I had since that first time, I now found that I was looking forward to the thought of it with some excited anticipation.

I shook my head at myself and frowned. I really needed to get my head out from the gutter. I threw on some comfortable clothes, dragged my hairbrush through my hair and then headed back downstairs to find Ryan in the kitchen, dishing up the food he'd cooked.

"Mmm, that smells delicious. What have you cooked for us this time?" I asked him, lifting my nose and inhaling the heavenly scent that floated in my direction.

"It's coq au vin. You know, chicken in wine. I wasn't sure if you would like it but thought I'd give it a go," Ryan replied, casting a smile in my direction quickly as he dished up the food.

"Well it looks and smells wonderful. I'm sure I'll love it," I informed him.

Leaving him to it, I ambled back into the living room, settling down upon the sofa and cocking my head when I noticed the television was paused, waiting for us to press play to continue whatever programme was on.

"What were you watching?" I called to Ryan, turning my head when he came into the room carrying two plates of food. He handed me one and then sat down on the sofa next to me. He picked up the remote control and pressed play before he answered me.

"I thought we could watch one of our period dramas that we both seem to love," he told me, just as the title sequence played across the screen.

I smiled warmly at him, thanking him for the food and for the film. I finally felt relaxed with things, feeling as though this was where I was meant to be with the person I was supposed to be with.

I couldn't wait for the date the following night.

CHAPTER SEVENTEEN.

Cal arrived home with a huge smile and lots of hugs and kisses for his daughter.

Lily giggled when she saw him, showing her excitement at seeing him after such a long time apart. Cal grinned at Ryan and myself when he eventually sat down with his daughter on his knee, holding her close to him as he asked us how the week had gone.

"It's been great," Ryan assured him, glancing to me for back up with what he'd said.

"Lily has been an absolute angel, Cal so you don't need to worry," I reassured him, smiling back at Ryan as I did so.

"And how about you two? Have you got any plans for the rest of your weekend now that you don't have to babysit?" Cal asked us both, seemingly delighted to be holding his daughter in his arms once more.

I glanced down sheepishly at that. Ryan could answer that question because I didn't want to. I heard Ryan clear his throat first.

"We're actually going on a date tonight, brother."

Cal stared at Ryan before shifting to stare at me,

the smile on his face getting even wider, even though I wasn't sure how that was physically possible.

"Finally!" Cal stated, "I'm glad you've decided to go for it!"

I could tell that he was aiming that last sentence at me but I refused to give him the satisfaction of seeing me acknowledge it. I didn't need to be told again that this was a good choice. I already knew it.

Apparently Ryan was a bit confused though.

"What do you mean Cal?"

"I mean, it's been blatantly obvious to the whole world that you two are into each other," Cal replied, not bothering to hide his laughter from us, "I'm glad you two are giving things a try. You're perfect for each other!"

"OK Cal, I get that you're happy about this but we've still got to go on a first date before you start saying we're perfect and all of that," I told him bashfully, tucking a strand of hair behind my ear.

As nice as it was to hear these things, it made me uncomfortable. I wasn't embarrassed but it was the same type of feeling.

"How was the tour?" I asked him then, hoping to change the subject. Thankfully, Cal took the hint and began to tell us all about his week away, meeting and greeting the fans that loved both him and Amber and how he'd signed a large number of books. He appeared to be very animated as he talked about the tour and I was ecstatic to him like it. I couldn't remember the last time I'd seen him look as happy as he was in that moment and I was pleased that it had been doing something that had included my sister. I knew that was most likely a big part of what had made him so happy because he'd wanted to get Amber's last words out into the world for so long.

We chatted for over an hour before Cal asked us what time our date was going to be at. When we said we hadn't decided on a time yet because we hadn't been sure what time he was going to be home, Cal ordered me to go home and get myself ready for my date and that Ryan would pick me up in an hour.

I laughed but didn't argue as I had been waiting for this date to happen all week long. I left and went home, choosing my outfit carefully. I felt like dressing sexily considering that it was a date but I didn't want to overdo it as I didn't know where we were going.

In the end, I chose a purple pencil skirt that ended just below my knees and a pale pink top with lacy embroidering over it and a low cut neckline. Paired with a pair of strappy high heels and some makeup on my face and I was ready to go.

I put my jacket on, covering myself up before I left the house because the air was nippy outside.

Ryan rang on my doorbell ten minutes later. I flung the door open, eager to see if he had dressed up and to my pleasure, he did not disappoint.

He was wearing a white shirt and pale blue trousers with a pale blue jacket which fit him perfectly. I knew he must have borrowed the suit from Cal but it suited him, making his grey eyes stand out as they glistened whilst he gazed at me. I heard his intake of breath.

"You look beautiful," he told me, holding his hand out for me as I stepped out of the house and locked the door. We hopped into his car.

"Thankyou, you look pretty hot yourself," I replied, blushing as I glanced at him. He thought I was beautiful and he'd not even seen my top! The jacket covered everything so he couldn't see my whole outfit. Yet.

"Where are we going?" I asked him after a few minutes, breaking the silence that had descended upon us.

"I was planning on taking you to a fancy Chinese restaurant that's not too far from here. You've probably been before but I'm hoping you like it all the same," he informed me, allowing me to see that he was nervous for just a moment.

I studied my surroundings as we approached the restaurant, my heart beating fast in my chest. I couldn't remember the last time I'd been on a date. With someone other than Jacob. As we pulled up outside of the restaurant, I knew which one it was. And Ryan had been right, it was one I had been to before and loved!

We walked inside the restaurant and were promptly shown to a table for two with candles already lit at the tables. I shucked off my jacket, hanging it over my chair and sat down, wriggling my bottom until I was comfortable.

When I looked back up, I noticed that Ryan was staring at me.

"What? What's wrong?" I asked, feeling self-conscious as he stared at me. He blinked, bringing his hand up to scrub it over his face.

"Do you know how stunning you look right now?" he asked me, his voice husky as his eyes remained on me. Oh, my top! I'd forgotten about that. I smiled shyly at him.

"I take it you like my top then?"

"I love your top," he answered, tearing his eyes away to glance back at my eyes, "it certainly compliments you."

"Thanks," I responded, picking up the menu to try and divert my attention so that I could choose my food.

*   *   *

The meal was superb and the conversation flowed easily between the two of us.

We stayed at the restaurant for a couple of hours as we savoured the scrumptious food and took our time as we got to know each other even more on our date.

I'd finally found my courage to ask Ryan what his job actually was. All I'd know up until that point was that he worked for a company that handled business with other companies and that he was quite high up in the business hierarchy but because I'd felt it wasn't any of my business I hadn't asked and nobody else had ever offered the information up to me freely. However, curiosity got the better of me at last so I asked.

I was gobsmacked by his answer as I discovered that he was actually the owner of the company, which in hindsight explained to me how he had managed to take time off pretty much whenever he wanted as he could delegate to his employees whilst he was away.

When Ryan had seen the astonishment on my face, he'd laughed and asked me why I seemed so surprised. I ended up telling him the truth, that I'd known he was clever but thought he was too laid back to be someone's boss, let alone owning a company.

We changed the subject then and after we finished the meal, he drove me home. As we pulled up outside of my rented house, I turned to him and invited him inside.

Naturally, he said yes. We'd both known this was most likely how the evening was going to end up already. I climbed out of the car and made my way to the front door to unlock it whilst Ryan followed me, locking the door behind us once we were inside.

I made my way to the kitchen so that I could get us both another drink and as I went, I found myself wanting to ask a question that I'd wanted to ask since I'd discovered the truth about his job.

"Ryan? Why did you never tell me about what your position is at work? Why has it always been such a secret?"

I pulled a can of lager out of the fridge for him and then poured myself a glass of wine. I glanced up to see Ryan tug nervously at his collar.

"I've found that when people know what I do, they tend to go for my money instead of getting to know me and I wanted to know that you liked me for me and not what I can make in a year," he admitted, a guilty expression on his face.

"I can understand that. I'd like to think that you would know that I'm not like that anyway but then, you didn't know me well enough to know better so I get it," I allowed, seeing things from his point of view, "but just so that we're clear, I don't care if you're rich or if you're poor. I like you and that's all that matters to me."

"I know," Ryan's voice came from right behind me as I'd turned to pick our drinks up. His hands slithered around my waist as his body pressed up against my back. My whole body sprang to life, instantly aware of his close proximity to me as he bent his head and pressed a gentle kiss to my neck. I tilted my head a little, angling my head so that he had better access to my neck as he began to nuzzle me there, his arms holding me tighter around my middle.

I raised my hand to catch a hold of the back of his head, running my fingers through his silky smooth hair as he nibbled along my jawline, his own hand lifting up to tilt my head backwards so that he could capture my mouth in his from the position he held from behind me.

I sighed contentedly into his mouth, even as he used his hands to swivel me around in his arms so that I could face him. He kissed me hungrily, the desire he held for me not even in question at this present time.

We kissed passionately for several minutes before

he lifted me up, sweeping me off of my feet and carrying me up the stairs into my bedroom. He stopped to gaze about him for a few seconds as it looked vastly different from when he had last seen it when I'd moved in. I'd made it all purple and silver in the colour scheme, attempting to make it appear cosy and magical at the same time. Judging by the gleam that appeared in Ryan's eyes, I felt confident that he approved of my bedroom.

Carrying me over to the bed, he placed me gently on the top of it before shrugging his jacket off of his shoulders and onto the floor. Then, he climbed onto the bed with me, taking my mouth in his once more as he trailed his fingers down my body with such a gentle caress that my body ached from the tenderness of it, arching into him as his mouth explored mine with a deepening kiss that was making me forget where I was.

I moaned into his mouth, my lust for him rising as his kisses didn't let up. I unbuttoned his shirt, sliding it off of his shoulders once the buttons were free of the nooses that held them in place, revealing to me his firm toned torso that I remembered clearly from our previous time in the bedroom. I trailed his muscles in wonder, their firmness causing goose pimples to appear along my arms.

Ryan pushed my top upwards then, murmuring how it would only be fair if mine disappeared also. He lifted the top over my head and threw it onto the floor to join his own by the side of the bed. A moment later and my bra joined them.

"Beautiful, just beautiful," he breathed huskily as he took in the sight of me below him on the bed, his eyes darkening as he gazed at me hungrily.

He descended upon me then, pressing kisses along my collarbone, travelling lower until he reached my breasts. He covered them with his hands as well as his mouth, working them to heighten my pleasure whilst being gentle and tender with me the entire time, ensuring that I could trust that I was safe in his arms.

He tugged at my skirt, hoping to pull it down but I stopped him, knowing I needed to undo the zip first.

"You take your own clothes off whilst I wrestle with my skirt," I whispered, chuckling a little when he groaned in frustration. He gave me a swift kiss on my lips before he stood up, breaking himself free of his trousers and boxers whilst I did the same with my skirt and underwear. Within minutes, he was back on top of me, his hardness pressing against my inner thigh.

I pointed at the foil packet that lay on the top of the small table next to the bed, indicating to him that he needed to put it on before we went any further.

He grinned and did what I wanted immediately,

kissing me as he fiddled with it until his hands came back up to my face, allowing me to know that he was ready.

"Are you ready for me?" he whispered into my ear, waiting for my response before he carried on.

His left hand reclaimed my breast, squeezing and tugging it when I breathed my answer into his ear.

"Yes."

He moved into me tenderly, attempting to be careful with me as he tried to take things slowly. I groaned in pleasure as I grabbed a hold of his bottom and urged him onwards, grateful when he picked up the speed as our passion grew rapidly between us.

It was as though we had been starved of each other, the tempo rising fast as our moans grew louder with each thrust. I could feel him getting closer, feeling my own desire reaching new heights until finally, I felt the burst of explosion within him, finding my own release at the same time as we hit our peaks together. Ryan gripped onto me tightly as he held us still, frozen until it was over. Eventually, Ryan panted and rolled off of me and over to the side, pulling me close against his body as he snuggled up to me in pure satisfaction. I grinned happily as I closed my eyes to fall asleep next to him.

CHAPTER EIGHTEEN.

Weeks passed and Ryan and I were happy.

I went to his some weekends and he came to mine but we were together for the majority of the time. I was in a small blissful bubble as I began to let Ryan into my heart and lowered the defences I'd put up a long time before.

One Friday night, Ryan was at my house when my phone started to ring. I picked it up and glanced at the screen to see who was calling me. I frowned when I saw the name. Placing the phone against my ear, I answered it in a cold tone.

"What do you want Jacob?"

I felt Ryan stiffen beside me, his hand coming to rest on my thigh as I glanced at him in frustration. Why the hell was my ex-husband calling me? We weren't together anymore.

"Hi, Ellen. How are you?" came the reply from the man who'd cheated on me.

"I'm fine Jacob. But you didn't answer my question, what do you want?" I asked him bluntly, not wanting to waste time on pleasantries.

"Right, yeah. So the reason I rang you," he began, unable to hide his nervousness even on the phone, "you remember Amelia? The woman you met at the store with me?"

I rolled my eyes before I replied to him.

"Of course I remember her. I found her in bed with you if you recall. What about her?"

I heard Jacob sigh and then clear his throat on the other end of the phone.

"Look, I'm just calling you because I figured you deserved to hear it from me before you heard it from someone else. Amelia and I are getting married."

I was stunned. I knew I'd moved on with Ryan and that Jacob had moved on with Amelia but I hadn't realised he would marry again so soon. I couldn't tell whether I was hurt or not but I knew I was shocked. Above all else.

"Wow. Well thanks for letting me know," I told him bluntly, ending the call quickly before he could say anything else.

Ryan was watching me, his face uncertain as he waited for me to fill him in on what had just occurred.

"So, my ex-husband is getting married again to the woman I found him in bed with," I informed him, reeling a little from the news.

Ryan's hand covered mine and he pulled me in close towards him.

"Are you alright?" he asked, concern lacing his voice as he brushed my hair with his free hand soothingly.

I sighed against his chest as I allowed him to encase me within the safety of his arms.

"I'm alright," I replied to him quietly, glancing up at his face, "but I'm surprised that he's getting married again so soon after the divorce. Honestly? He can do whatever he wants. I don't care. And besides, I have you now so I'm not wasting any more time on Jacob. He's my ex and he's big enough and ugly enough to make his own mistakes."

Ryan chuckled at that, lifting my chin up to press a tender kiss to my lips.

"Can't say fairer than that," he muttered, "now how's about we have some fun tonight before you spend the whole weekend studying for your exam on Monday?"

I smiled against his lips, turning around to face him as the idea of a fun night filled my mind.

*   *   *

I had spent the rest of that weekend studying for my A-level exam that I had been working all year for and then when the Monday finally arrived, I felt quietly confident that I would pass this test.

I had already applied to my university of choice being as the exam had finally gotten as close as it had and they'd informed me that I would be accepted onto the course I had chosen, depending upon the result I received in this exam. So there was an awful lot riding on this exam and whether I passed or not.

I sat the exam, spending the hours I had to complete the exam and then going over it all to double-check my answers whilst I still had the time. I thought that I perhaps had passed but after taking the exam, my confidence wasn't as great as when I'd started. I could only hope and pray that I'd passed because then I could go on to university and get my nursing degree.

*   *   *

"I did it! I got in!" I squealed as I opened the letter I'd just received from the university.

I'd not long heard that I had passed my A-level exam and now, in my hand I was holding onto my letter of acceptance from the university, informing me that I officially had a place on the nursing course that I had opted for.

I ran over to Ryan and jumped on him, thanking the heavens that he didn't drop me as I laughed and kissed him in my excitement. Ryan laughed along with me as he shifted his arms to hold onto me tighter so that I couldn't fall.

"Congratulations! I'd ask if you were happy about it but it's kinda obvious," he chuckled as I hugged him tightly.

I beamed a huge smile at him as I let go of him and allowed him to lower me back down onto the ground. I felt like a child that had just been given the best present in the world.

"Eek! I want to celebrate!" I squealed, still bouncing around as I waved the letter in my hands happily, "shall we call Cal and see if he and Lily want to do something?"

Ryan laughed at me, his eyes softening as he gazed at me. I loved it when he looked at me that way. It made me feel like I was the only woman for him.

"Yeah that sounds like a great idea," he told me as he caught a hold of my hand and pulled me back towards him, his lips crashing against mine in a hungry manner.

Several hours later and we were sat in a local pub having a meal together whilst Lily played with the children's toys that they had. Cal had agreed to come out with us as soon as I told him my good news and he had wanted to help us to celebrate.

We were all eating our food when Cal began a new conversation.

"So I know you've changed your shifts around so that you can cover your bills and everything, but Ryan and I have been discussing things about how we can help you out," he said, idly playing with one of the toys that Lily had picked up. That piqued my interest.

"Oh yeah? Like what?" I asked them, taking a sip of my drink as I glanced at first Cal and then Ryan.

Ryan smiled as he gestured for Cal to continue with what he was saying which made my curiosity ratchet up a few notches.

"Well, if you agree of course, Ryan and I would like to take care of your bills so that you don't have to work whilst you're at university. We have the money between us to be able to afford it and you are family so we would very much like to make this endeavour of yours just that little bit easier," Cal told me, taking a deep breath as he waited for my answer.

I stared open mouthed at him, then turned to Ryan with a questioning gaze to which he nodded his head to confirm what had just been said. I was dumbfounded.

"What? I can't accept that," I spluttered, shocked that they'd offered to help me in such a way. It was very nice of them but I'd always had to make my own way in life before. Even my ex-husband hadn't helped me like that.

"It's not forever, Ellen. It's just whilst you're studying because we've done our own research and you would be constantly working or studying with no life of your own and we didn't see the point in you working yourself into the ground when we have the means to make things easier for you," Cal told me, smiling warmly at me.

I was at a loss for words. What could I say to that?

"How's about you think about it for a few days and then let us know? I know it's a lot to take in right now but we truly do just want the best for you," Ryan told me, covering my hand with his as I glanced between the two of them.

I nodded my head in agreement, pondering over their suggestion as I shovelled some food into my mouth. It would be very nice to do as they suggested but I didn't want to be beholden to them so maybe I could still work a couple of shifts so that I had some money of my own instead of being a kept woman.

I was certainly too independent for that nonsense.

CHAPTER NINETEEN.

I started university with every ounce of me jumping for joy as I settled down on that first day to learn what I needed to to become a nurse.

I made several new friends during those first few weeks which certainly helped, especially when some of them were near to my age. I'd originally thought that I would be the oldest person there but I had soon been proved wrong and how glad was I that that was the case.

I'd also taken Cal and Ryan up on their offer for financial support on the condition that I still worked two nights a week after I'd finished university so that I could still contribute to paying for things without feeling guilty every time I spent money. If it was my own money, then I wouldn't feel guilty.

In order for Ryan to pay for the bills without having to pay his own bills for his flat, we had had a very serious discussion and decided that it would be best for him to move in with me. I wasn't certain that it was the best thing for us but it would be a good way to discover if we could live together. He'd moved in to my house about a month after I started university which I found worked out quite well for us and I had to admit that it was fantastic knowing that I could go home and discuss my day with the man I shared my life with and he was actually interested in what I had to say.

Ryan informed me of his job at his business, finally telling me all about it because he felt that he could trust me. He'd wanted me to fall in love with him for him and not his money which I had, which was why he'd offered to help me financially but he'd known I might take offense if he'd done it by himself which was where Cal had come into it. They knew if they shared the load between them, I would be more likely to say yes. Plus the fact that I still wanted to work a little to have some money of my own had apparently gone a long way in making Ryan feel even more secure about us. He knew I wasn't going to use him or take him for a ride.

I was four months into my university course when I started being sick every day. I couldn't explain it. I would be sick in the morning, feel groggy all day and then it would start all over again the next day.

This went on for a couple of weeks before I called up Eva for a distraction one weekend. Ryan had gone to work for the morning, leaving me to my own devices. Ryan hadn't wanted to go in due to my constant sickness but I told him to go and that I would take care of myself. After all, I'd managed to go to my classes each day. I'd be sick and then carry on as normal, whilst feeling queasy throughout.

Broken Tulips

I'd sat watching rubbish on the television for the morning but after I'd received a text message from Eva, I decided to call her and chat. I knew if someone could cheer me up then she would.

"Hi Eva!" I greeted as she picked up on the other end.

"Ellen! Hey, it's good to hear from you," she replied brightly, "actually I'm glad you called, I've got something to tell you!"

"Oh yeah? What's that then?" I asked her, smiling as she got straight to telling me the gossip.

"Do you remember Jack? Well, we're seeing each other now. You were totally right! I don't know what I was so scared of!" she cried down the phone, giggling to let me know her excitement.

"I knew it! I knew you would get on well together."

I smiled to myself, thinking about when I'd gone to see her and the fact that they had been interested in each other from before then. It was about time they'd gotten together. I paused. I suddenly realised how everyone else had felt about Ryan and myself when we'd gotten together. It had been a long time coming.

"I know!" she squealed happily, "anyway, enough about me. You still feeling poorly?"

I grunted at that. I'd mentioned it to her when we had been messaging each other and I should've realised that she'd bring it up now.

"Yeah, still being sick. I've decided to go to the doctors next week being as it hasn't passed. I thought it would go away by itself but it doesn't seem to be going anywhere," I replied glumly, sighing to myself.

I heard Eva take a sharp intake of breath before she continued.

"Have you thought about the fact that you might be pregnant?"

"What?!" I exclaimed, horror washing over me as I started to think about it even as Eva tried to convince me.

"Yeah, think about it. You're sick in the mornings, you feel rubbish all day long. Take a test to find out. You never know, it might not be that but it's always best to rule it out right?"

I swore under my breath and said a hurried goodbye to Eva. She was right. I needed to take a test to find out if this was indeed down to being pregnant.

I ran out to my car and hopped in, driving to the nearest shop that would sell pregnancy tests. Minutes later and I was back home, running up the stairs and reading the instructions on the test packaging before I went ahead with it.

Once I was certain that I knew what I was doing, I took the test and then waited the recommended time before I picked it up to see what it said.

Pregnant.

Oh God, I was pregnant! That was why I was being sick! I groaned to myself as horrified realisation washed over me, my hands shaking as I held the test in them.

I sat there unmoving for several minutes when I heard a car door slam outside, followed by the door to my house being opened.

"Ellen! I'm home!" Ryan called out, announcing his presence.

I swallowed hard as I glanced back down at the test in my hands. I was going to have to tell him. How did I tell someone that I was pregnant when I was horrified by the thought?

I stood up weakly, taking a deep breath before making my way down the stairs. I found Ryan in the kitchen, making himself a cup of tea when he turned around to face me. Seeing the expression on my face, he hurried over to me with a look of concern on his features.

"Ellen? What's wrong?" he asked me furtively, coming to a stop right in front of me.

"I've found out why I'm being sick," I muttered, holding up the pregnancy test for him to see for himself.

He took it from me, glancing down at the test

in confusion until a moment later, realisation dawned on him. He whipped his head back up at me.

"You're pregnant?"

"Yeah, looks like it," I sighed, going over to one of the chairs nearby and sinking into it wearily.

"But this is great news!" he cried out, coming over to me and kneeling down so that we were at eye level, a huge smile spread across his face.

I looked at him incredulously.

"You think so? We've not even been together a year, I'm studying at university and I'm pregnant! This wasn't what I had planned on us dealing with just yet," I snapped, unable to hide the fear that had risen within me.

His smile faltered as he studied me, realising that I wasn't as happy as he was by the news.

"I know it's unexpected Ellen but we can deal with this. There will surely be maternity leave that you can take at university as they wouldn't be allowed not to have it in place. And in regards to us, do you think we are likely to break up?" he asked me softly, his hand resting upon my knee.

My shoulders slumped as I contemplated my answer.

"No, I'd like to think that we won't," I admitted, "but how do I know for sure? Look at what happened with me and Jacob."

Ryan frowned at me then. I knew he didn't like it when I spoke about Jacob but it was necessary to be said.

"Do you truly think I am anything like Jacob?" he asked me, unable to hide his displeasure at being likened to Jacob.

"No, of course I don't. I'm just saying that we don't know what will happen."

Ryan pondered my response for a few seconds, frowning as he did so. He knew I was right.

"OK, you're right about that. But do you really want to get rid of our beautiful baby? Especially when things could work out fantastically between us and we could have a beautiful little family? I'm personally ecstatic to find out you're pregnant but I understand your trepidation. It is your decision what we do here, Ellen and I promise that I will support you with whichever decision you make," he told me, wrapping his arms around me into a gentle hug.

I needed to think. Could I get rid of my baby? Or could I work things out that I would keep the child and see if Ryan and myself could last? There was a lot to think about all of a sudden and it filled me with dread.

EPILOGUE.

Nine months later.

"Push! Push! Come on, you can do it!"

The nurse overseeing my birth shouted the words to me but all I could focus on was the pain of pushing this child out of me. Ryan was in the room with us, letting me hold his hand as I squeezed with all of my might.

Judging by the look of pain on his face, I guessed I was probably squeezing too hard but damn it! I was in pain pushing this baby out and he should know at least a small portion of that pain too! It was his fault I was here after all.

I screamed as I continued to push, doing what the nurse said and breathing in between. I was feeling worn out already as we had been at this for five hours. I truly hoped my child would arrive soon.

I was looking forward to meeting her but I also wanted this excruciating pain to be over. Everyone kept telling me that once the baby was born and I gazed upon her, I would forget all about this pain but at the way I felt in that moment, I couldn't believe that it was true. How could anyone ever forget this pain?

I'd decided to keep the baby, allowing Ryan and myself to take a chance on having a family together, even though I had thought it would be a bad idea but Ryan had been great throughout the whole pregnancy. He'd found out everything to do with maternity leave at the university for me and had gone with me for every meeting with both the hospital and the university. Luckily, I was able to take a pause in my course, returning in one year so that I could pick up right where I left off which I was utterly grateful for.

Ryan had gotten me every comfort, every product for a baby that we could think of and had even bought me crate loads of orange tango drinks as that was what I had craved throughout the pregnancy.

I had gotten larger with each passing month, growing so huge that it was difficult to do every day things. After getting extremely frustrated one day, Ryan had treated me to a spa day at home. It had included him giving me massages and a hot relaxing bath whilst waiting on me hand and foot for the day to make me feel better.

I knew I was an extremely lucky woman to have a man in my life who would do that sort of thing, especially considering how crabby I had been lately. My hormones had been all over the place and I knew I had been horrible to live with but Ryan had been a gentleman about it all, constantly remaining nice to me, holding me in the night when I'd burst into random tears at the state my body had gotten into. He continued to tell me that I was beautiful and that he would love me always.

Another hour and a half passed when she finally arrived.

My beautiful baby girl. She arrived in the world at 3:04pm weighing in at 5lb 2oz.

I cried with relief at her arrival, turning to Ryan as he watched the nurses cut the umbilical cord and wrap her up into a blanket so that we could hold her at last.

The nurse handed her over to me with a smile on her face.

"Congratulations, you've got a beautiful baby girl," she announced. I was so happy to see the small bundle in my arms that I began to cry even more.

Ryan pressed a gentle kiss against my forehead, brushing my hair away from my forehead.

"She's beautiful. Just like her mum," he whispered into my ear, leaning in close to us as we took a good look at our daughter.

She was perfect. I smiled down at her in my arms as I held her close, observing her tiny fingers in her tiny hand, her eyes closed as she wriggled around in my grasp.

I glanced up at Ryan to see his face. He was gazing down adoringly at our perfect new addition to our little family.

"Can we still call her what we agreed? Are you still ok with it?" I asked him quietly, hoping that he hadn't changed his mind. In my eyes, the name suited her perfectly and I didn't want to have to choose another name.

"Yes, of course I still agree. And I'm sure Cal will be pleased to hear it. I'm going to ring him and let him know that he can come and visit you now if that's alright? He's been so worried about you."

"Thanks Ryan. I'd love for him to meet our baby girl. Let's hope Lily likes her too," I supplied, chuckling at the idea of my niece getting jealous of her cousin.

Ryan made the phone call as I gazed at my daughter, smiling down at her as I realised that I was very happy that we'd decided to keep her.

We didn't have to wait long for Cal to arrive. Ten minutes later and he was walking through the door to my ward, bringing Lily with him.

"That was quick!" I exclaimed in surprise as I watched the man walk over to us.

"We were just downstairs in the cafeteria," Cal informed me as he gave me a quick hug then turned to give his brother a hug.

"Ah ok," I allowed, "well, we would like for you to meet our daughter. We've decided to name her Amber."

I saw the look of surprise mixed with sadness on his face as he looked from me to Ryan. I knew the ache that he held inside of him for my sister and I'd hoped that he would be happy with our choice of name for our daughter. I wanted to honour my sister by naming my daughter after her aunt.

Cal kissed me on the cheek, gazing down lovingly at our daughter with a tear in his eye.

"That's really lovely," he said, swiping at his face to dash the tear away, "look Lily, this is your cousin Amber!"

He lifted his child up so that she could see the baby.

She smiled and stuck her tongue out at me playfully, something I had unfortunately taught her but it made me chuckle.

Ryan came over to us at the side of the bed, clearing his throat and starting to appear a bit nervous.

"Being as you're all here, there's something else that I'd like to do," he said, sitting on the edge of the bed with me and taking one of my hands into his.

Cal and I stole a quick glance at each other, wondering what Ryan was up to now. When I turned my attention back to Ryan, he was pulling something from his pocket and holding it up to me.

"I love you Ellen and you're now the mother of my child. I can't think of anyone that I would rather spend my life with and I want to spend it with you. Will you do me the honour of becoming my wife?"

I stared at him in shock. He was proposing to me! This gorgeous hunk of a man who had fathered the beautiful little girl in my arms was asking me to marry him! I did the only thing that I could.

"Yes!"

AUTHOR NOTE.

I would like to say a special thankyou to everybody that has supported me on my writing journey so far.

I started writing at a very young age and both of my parents encouraged me to read and write as much as possible. They were brilliant and as they are no longer with me, this whole trilogy of books is for them. Blue roses are in memory of my dad and forget me nots are in memory of my mum. Due to the fact that I had started using a flower theme in this set of books, I decided to continue it with the tulips for this book.

I also would like to say thank you to my family and friends who have shown their support for me throughout this year, including a family friend named Karen who gave me the locations in Devon that I have used in this book. Thankyou Karen!

I truly enjoy writing these books and I hope that you are all enjoying reading them. If you would like to follow me on Facebook, simply type in Author Julie Thorpe in the search engine to keep up to date with all things new with me!

Thank you again for your continued support, it truly means everything to me.

From Julie x

Printed in Great Britain
by Amazon